PERSONAL INDIANAPOLIS

Thirteen Years of Observing, Exhorting, and Satirizing the Hoosier Capital

DAVID HOPPE

Hawthorne Publishing

ISBN: 978-0-9912095-4-5

Photo credits:

David Hoppe photo courtesy Duncan Alney
City of Indianapolis: iStock/Aneese/www.thinkstock.com
Newspapers: Wavebreak Media/Wavebreakmedia
Ltd/www.thinkstock.com

Hawthorne Publishing
15601 Oak Road
Carmel, Indiana 46033
www.hawthornepub.com
317-867-5183

DEDICATION

For Melli
and for Graham:
there from the start

Introduction

Over his thirteen years as a commentator for a scrappy Indianapolis newsweekly that prides itself on roughness around the edges, David Hoppe never has stopped challenging his readers to be Renaissance men and women.

For his erstwhile fellow NUVO columnists Steve Hammer and Harrison Ullmann reveled in the take-no-prisoners m.o., David prefers to round up friends and enemies alike and transport them to re-education camps with sunny weather and hearty meals to go with the stern but engrossing lectures.

"The poet William Blake once wrote words to the effect that we never know what's enough until we experience too much," he writes in one of the specimens collected in this book. "That is probably true. But the problem with defining freedom in terms of our excesses is that it substitutes imaginative impoverishment for genuine abundance. It doesn't take imagination to keep doing the same thing again and again until exhaustion sets in. On the other hand, a creative leap is required to envision all that might be possible should we set about trying something really new."

What's perennially new to consumers of typical media punditry is Hoppe's brand: original, adventurous thinking, graced with erudition, backed with research, lit with anger at fools and bullies, and assembled with seamless rhetorical economy and elegance. Ability to operate on such a plane takes a journalist and then some, which Hoppe is. He's a fiction writer, a playwright, a former library director and administrator of arts and humanities. A culture vulture, Midwestern bred, and proud of it.

As a bona fide public intellectual for our times, Hoppe insists that the workaday business of newspapers—partisan politics, pollution, poverty, prejudice and, yes, sports and sex—can be raised to the level of literature and infused with larger meaning without overtaxing or alienating a citizen who'd never picture himself in Hoppe's circle of cognoscenti.

How, after all, can one feel talked down to by a confessed follower of baseball's perennial champions of heartbreak?

"Cub fans," he writes, "have had to find ways to cope with this ongoing drought that taps deep into our psyches. There's something existential about it. Bill Murray said it best after the team imploded during the 2003 playoffs. According to Murray, Cubs fans had lived through losing before and knew how to deal with it. 'We are not like the others,' he said."

That particular column traces Hoppe's passion for the game and his team back to his suburban Chicago boyhood and his true-believer dad; it's one of many droll and touching examples of his penchant for pairing the personal with the profound, as this book's title implies. His anecdotes about life with wife Melli, son Graham and others close to him make for tasty reading as human interest features—yet they often serve as levers for heavy lifting in the bargain.

"The first thing that hit us when we walked through the door at the nursing home where my mom spent the past summer was the claustrophobic smell of unflushed urine," a singularly powerful column opens. "That's what you get when you pack several hundred human beings who are too weak or off balance to take care of themselves in a single building with low ceilings and crowded hallways."

Sure, many of us can relate. But there's more. Hoppe goes on to point out that Indiana ranked notoriously low in federally measured standards of care for the institutionalized elderly and disabled.

"It's been said that Indiana doesn't take good care of its kids. Well, the situation is worse if you're old." The message: Don't just empathize with the author and his subjects; use your vote and your voice to reform what he's exposed.

Exposing the naked emperor is a Hoppe specialty, whether it's "fiscally responsible" government that neglects basic services, the aristocracy of welfare capitalists or a revered but compromised elected official. Likewise ripe for ambush are complacent liberals who might fancy themselves a choir to which their compadre will reliably preach. In the renegade spirit of Henry David Thoreau, who prayed "May I always disappoint my friends," the high-minded Hoppe clearly doesn't give a damn whether he always pleases them. And thus, he rarely disappoints, as this compilation of greatest hits attests. I know he would much rather I could say so about his beloved Cubs—World Champs, 1908!—but I proudly extend him this consolation prize all the same. *Personal Indianapolis* is less overdue than they, but only by a century give or take a few years.

Dan Carpenter

Preface

Columnists are made, not born.

When my NUVO colleague and editor Jim Poyser first broached the idea of my writing a regular column, I ducked. I had been chipping in the occasional opinion piece for the paper, but the prospect of doing it on a weekly basis was daunting.

Jim, bless his heart, wouldn't let go of the idea and, years later, we have this book.

NUVO is what is called an alternative weekly. The alternative press as we have come to know it got its start in the 1960's. It covered what was called the counter-culture and gave voice to ideas, perspectives and opinions given short shrift by the mainstream media.

The need for this kind of journalism has never been satisfied. In fact, that need may be more acute than ever. In any event, I have no doubt that without a venue like NUVO, a column like mine wouldn't exist.

For me, the platform provided by the alternative approach has always been liberating. It's an opportunity to consider any and all issues, but without the reductive and often arbitrary framing that corporate media often seems compelled to impose. This freedom creates, I think, a special obligation to try and find connections, dimensions and, if nothing else, a slightly different way of writing about issues and events that are finding their way into peoples' lives.

What a lucky break, then, for a writer like me to find himself living in Indianapolis, a city with an alternative weekly that practically defines the form. Thanks to the vision and downright stubbornness of its publisher and editor-in-chief Kevin McKinney, NUVO continues to be locally owned and completely independent, qualities that are increasingly rare, even among the ranks of supposedly alternative papers.

There are, of course, more ways of getting the word out available to people than ever before. Anyone can post an opinion, idea or critique in the electronic ether and, sometimes, even find an audience. The impact on media in general and journalism, in particular, has been momentous and continues.

But the role of publications like NUVO—whether on paper, or in an electronic incarnation—in contributing to its community's distinct sense of identity, is still crucial.

Writing a column every week turns out, for this writer anyway, to be a dream gig. The thought of it may once have made me duck; I got over that in no time.

January 2014
Long Beach, Indiana

"Ain't God Good to Indiana? Ain't He, fellers, ain't He, though?"

A perambulation around Hoosier poet William Herschell's deathless question, exploring the state's culture, sense of place, and political peccadilloes…John Dillinger, Richard Lugar, Peyton Manning, and Kurt Vonnegut all make appearances.

Terrorism...or Tourism:
A Terrorist's Guide to the Hoosier State
July 19, 2006

The folks down at Indiana Homeland Security must have been imbibing William Herschell's paean to the Hoosier state when they set about the task of identifying sites that need to be protected from terrorist attack: "Ain't God good to Indiana? Ain't He, fellers, Ain't He, though?"

It seems that as part of our country's permanent War on Terror, all the states and territories were asked to come up with a list of potential terrorist targets for inclusion in a federal asset database. This exercise had a quality of free play about it, in that the Feds refrained from giving local homeland security officials specific guidelines about what might or might not be included on such a list.

Indiana, it's been said, is a state that suffers from a kind of collective low self-esteem. "Why would you want to move here?" is a question that often dogs people who relocate to our state from places with mountains or seacoasts like California, Colorado, or Florida. So you might have been forgiven for thinking that drawing up a list of local targets wouldn't have taken our homeland protectors much time. I mean, in a world as dangerous as this one has become, it's always seemed to me that Indiana's biggest asset was its lack of, well, assets. In other words, why would a terrorist want to come here?

It turns out there are plenty of reasons—8,591 of them, to be exact. And these were just the ones the federal government was willing to accept. Our homeland security officials were able to think of a couple thousand sites and events on top of that, but they were told this constituted an embarrassment of riches. Evidently we were making New York and Virginia feel bad.

When you think about it, this is really kind of sweet.

1

Indiana chose to identify more potential terrorist targets than any other state or territory. Once our homeland security folks started thinking about it, it seems there wasn't anyplace in Indiana that wasn't sacred. Although the actual list is still a secret, enough information has been leaked for us to know that it includes a popcorn maker, an ice cream parlor, a casket company, several Wal-Marts, a tackle shop, some nightclubs, a brewery and, thank goodness, a donut shop. "Every disaster is a local disaster," said Pam Bright, spokeswoman for the Indiana Department of Homeland Security, giving new meaning to our Hoosier sense of place. "We knew how we came up with our list. We looked at it in the other direction: Why wouldn't the other [states] have more?"

Of course, it must be admitted that we Hoosiers are a rather fearful people. An inch of snow is enough to make us want to stock up on canned goods and bottled water, and the very idea of marriage between anybody but a man and woman sends shivers down our serially monogamous spines. Indiana was one state that had a terrorism preparedness plan in place before September 11, 2001.

But we are proud. And so our list of agricultural assets leaves Illinois and Minnesota in the dust. Our 5,456 public health assets account for two-thirds the national total. The terrorists will know we honor our elders: we put 417 nursing homes on our list of possible targets.

Chicago may have the Hancock Building and the Sears Tower; Manhattan can brag about the Empire State Building. But we love our tall buildings, too. It may come as news to terrorists that we have forty-one of these mighty monuments, thirteen more than are listed by Illinois.

It just goes to show you that there is more than corn in Indiana. While we can't know exactly what's on the official list of sites in need of protection, I suspect that every Hoosier has a list that comes to mind, a personal Indiana, as it were, that's deserving of attention and that, were the unthinkable to happen, would forever compromise whatever it is we think of when we think of Hoosier-ness.

For example, no such list would be complete without Michigan City's Blue Chip Casino. Where else can you lose $100 in less than twenty minutes? Then, in Huntington, there's the Dan Quayle Museum honoring the former vice president whose debating style columnist Charles Krauthammer described as "shrill and annoying." And he was a fan.

There are towns with evocative names like Santa Claus, Buddha, Surprise, Bobtown, and Bud. In Peru one finds the Circus Hall of Fame and a favorite drive-in where they ladle chili into an open sack of Fritos and call it a "walking taco."

Let's hope that, from now on, an extra detachment of security will be discreetly assigned to the annual Mint Festival in North Judson.

Let terrorists note: as William Herschell wrote—and the Indiana Department of Homeland Security has so generously affirmed: "Other spots may look as fair, But they lack th' soothin' somethin' in th' Hoosier sky and air…They don't know th' joys of Heaven have their birthplace here below; Ain't God good to Indiana? Ain't He fellers? Ain't He, though?"

The Third Coast: It's Our Lake, Too
August 15, 2012

I had my eyes opened last week.

My wife and I and a couple of friends of ours went on a road trip. We started in Michigan City, Indiana, and drove up the Michigan coast to the point where Lake Michigan meets another of the Great Lakes, Huron, at the Straits of Mackinac.

Those of us living in central Indiana can easily forget that part of this state's northern edge is bordered by an inland sea. For us, the

Indiana landscape tends to be flat, all the better for planting acre upon acre of corn and soybeans. Most of our water comes from rivers and streams, or manmade reservoirs and wells.

It's no wonder, then, that so many of us, upon first laying eyes on Lake Michigan, are liable to blurt out something to the effect that this sure doesn't feel like Indiana.

Lake Michigan gets its name from the Ojibwa Indians; it is believed to be a derivation of *mishigami*, or great water. The lake has a surface area of 22,400 square miles, making it the fifth largest lake in the world, and the most expansive to be found entirely within one country. Its deepest point is 923 feet, and it offers 1,640 miles of shoreline.

Our friends, being new to the area, had thought they could drive around the lake—it was just a lake, after all—in an afternoon. They got as far as the suburbs north of Chicago before realizing they were over-matched.

I, on the other hand, spent a large part of my growing up on Lake Michigan beaches. I'd seen twelve- and fourteen-foot waves, heard the stories about shipwrecks. I thought I understood something about the lake's scale. But I had never seen the lake from its uppermost point. This was a revelation.

In central Indiana, when we want to feel a sense of space, we tend to look up. The sky provides us with evidence of something more expansive than ourselves. On Lake Michigan, you not only look up, you look out. The sheer vastness of it, the distance to the horizon, where the water meets the sky, is breathtaking.

At the Straits of Mackinac, where an elegant suspension bridge connects the northern tip of Michigan's mitten with the Upper Peninsula, you experience this by looking either west, across Lake Michigan, or east toward Lake Huron. On the map, this point looks like a punctuation mark. Maps, though, often bear little resemblance to the landscapes they are meant to describe. In person, the magnitude of the strait is at once humbling and exhilarating. It can change the way you think about being a midwesterner.

The most beautiful view we found was from atop a four-hundred-foot bluff along the Sleeping Bear Dunes, about a thirty-minute drive west of Traverse City. The day we were there, sunlight turned the lake into massive bands of aquamarine and indigo. On the beach at Sleeping Bear Point, looking out to the islands of North and South Manitou, the rocks were rounded smooth and the bright, clear water shimmered around our ankles.

The lake, of course, is not only a wonderful spiritual presence. It is a valuable resource. As Duke Energy's CEO Jim Rogers told *Forbes* magazine's Ken Silverstein last May, "Water is the new oil." If those of us living in central Indiana didn't know this before, we do now. This summer's historic drought has underscored the dependence of our state's way of life on its water supply.

As Silverstein wrote, "Energy production is water-intensive and the vast supplies that are needed to run every type of power plant—natural gas, coal, nuclear and renewables—is not well understood." According to the World Policy Institute, coal- and oil-fired power plants, like the ones we are so reliant upon in Indiana, consume twice the water of gas-fired facilities, but use less water than nuclear plants. Corn-based biofuels like ethanol consume greater amounts of water than drilling for traditional oil.

It's no wonder there's a large coal-burning plant beside the harbor in Michigan City. Or that oil giant BP has one of the nation's largest oil refineries located on the lake in Whiting, Indiana.

It behooves Hoosiers, in whatever part of the state they live, to think of Lake Michigan as part of who they are. It's our freshwater legacy, something that helps give shape to an understanding of what it means to be from this part of the Midwest.

But it may also prove to be our state's most important asset. How we treat Lake Michigan, and whether we are willing to stand up for its health and preservation, could determine what kind of state Indiana will be for years to come.

David Hoppe

Gangsters, Guns, and Gasoline: A Midwestern Sense of Place
May 3, 2010

Those who think that the Midwest is a place where nothing of note really happens should spend a little time perusing a book called *Public Enemies: America's Greatest Crime Wave and the Birth of the FBI, 1933-34* by Bryan Burrough. They'll be taken aback.

The first thing you realize when you read this book is that there are two kinds of history. There's the kind that tells the stories of everyday people doing what they must to get by. This is the kind, albeit punctuated with glimpses of the occasional Indian fight or cavalry raid, that seems to be preferred in Indiana. It focuses on settlement, clearing the land, planting crops, and building factories. According to this version of history, the emergence of a middle class is the biggest thing to ever happen here. That, and high school basketball, of course.

The other kind of history acknowledges these things, but its penchant is for character and incident. Growing up in the Midwest, I can remember feeling envious toward my peers who lived in states where the great events of the Revolution, say, or the Civil War, took place. I could only imagine what it must be like to come from Texas or Arizona, where the stories of gunfighters and lawmen were practically part of the landscape. This was a kind of history that had as much to do with storytelling as textbooks. It was history in Technicolor instead of black and white.

Bryan Burrough's *Public Enemies* belongs in this latter category. Weighing in at close to six hundred pages, including notes and bibliography, it is an epic tale stuffed with a truly wild cast of characters and more action than a spaghetti western. Except that it takes place here, which, I suppose, makes it a mid-western.

The story Burrough tells is set in the bleak heart of the Great Depression. There was massive unemployment; many Americans were just scraping by. The president, Franklin Roosevelt, was trying to use the federal government as a tool to breathe life into the country's exhausted economy on a national scale.

These conditions spawned a kind of outlaw that was seemingly peculiar to the Midwest. He was working class or small town, and, thanks to the automobile, remarkably mobile. The characters that instigated what Burrough calls "America's Greatest Crime Wave" drove compulsively throughout a broad geographic corridor running from St. Paul, Minnesota, south through Illinois and Indiana, and down into Texas. They kidnapped the occasional tycoon, robbed banks all over the place, and killed people.

The stories of the Barker Gang, Baby Face Nelson, and, especially, Bonnie and Clyde and John Dillinger, have been told in various ways through separate biographies and, most notably, films. What makes *Public Enemies* different is that Burrough weaves all their stories together, which not only provides us with a heightened sense of the time period, but of the geography where they operated.

Indiana figures prominently. This is largely because of Dillinger, who grew up in Mooresville, robbed his first bank in Indianapolis, had fabled adventures in Crown Point and Michigan City, and is buried in Crown Hill Cemetery. By 1934, the second year of his crime spree, Dillinger achieved a national notoriety that's hard to imagine today. He was front-page news across the country and written up in *Time* magazine. When a Boy Scout visiting the governor of Indiana was asked by a reporter what he thought of Dillinger, the boy replied, "I'm for him…I mean, I'm always for the underdog."

The kid's reaction spoke to Dillinger's gift for theater. Quick with a quip or a dramatic gesture, Dillinger was an early master of media manipulation. His escapes, although more often due to the incompetence of law enforcement than his own ingenuity, were legendary.

Burrough takes pains to emphasize that Dillinger and his ilk

7

weren't heroes. Most were nasty, brutish, and not very bright. But there was also a desperation about them that resonated with people then, and still does today. Get off the interstate and drive through the small towns bisected by any of our state highways and, like as not, you'll be traveling through country that would have been familiar to Dillinger or the Barker Gang.

Although they occasionally robbed banks in larger urban centers, these crooks typically hit banks in smaller towns and used big cities as places to hide out. In this, as in their taste for flashy clothes, reliance on the Thompson submachine gun, and dependence on the automobile as trusty steed, they began to trace an outline that would soon become recognizable as an iconic part of modern America.

J. Edgar Hoover benefited from this. He used these criminals as justification to build a federal crime-fighting unit capable of crossing state lines. That unit became the FBI. Throughout the course of his career, Hoover kept the story of what happened in 1933 and 1934 under wraps so that he could create and promulgate his organization's creation myth. The recent release of the files from this period has provided scholars with a treasure trove of new insight into how things happened—and made Burrough's hefty book possible.

So get a copy and read *Public Enemies*. Then go for a drive. The Midwest may never feel the same to you again.

No State for Old People: Indiana's Nursing Home Disgrace
January 14, 2009

The first thing that hit us when we walked through the door at the nursing home where my mom spent the past summer was the claustrophobic smell of unflushed urine. That's what you get when you pack several hundred human beings who are too weak or off balance to take care of themselves in a single building with low ceilings and crowded hallways.

My mom, who turned eighty while she was there, has a diabetic condition that's caused her to lose the feeling in her feet. This makes it hard for her to walk and, in April, she tripped on the lip of a handicap ramp—yes, something supposed to make life easier for people like her—as she was trying to get in to see an exhibition about a local architect at the art center in Michigan City. The fall broke her leg in three places just below the knee. This necessitated surgery and the implementation of an excruciatingly painful steel contraption, like something out of a torture porn movie, pinning her leg together from the outside. Mom's doctor said the Russians developed this device under battlefield conditions during World War II. This was not exactly reassuring.

When the subject of nursing homes came up, nurses in the hospital where mom was being treated told her they wouldn't want to be stuck in any of the facilities in Michigan City. A place in another town, a few miles away, was recommended. This would mean driving an extra twenty minutes or so each way, but my dad, eighty-four, loves to drive, so this didn't seem like a problem.

This was our introduction to the world euphemistically known as elder care. Sounds and images come to mind: The hallway traffic jams of despondent or confused men and women in wheelchairs. Raspy voices crying out through different doorways for help or attention. The little crowd of aides who were always gathered outside the supply room to smoke cigarettes near my mom's window.

And, I should add, the daily kindnesses and, when called for, the forthrightness that many of those same aides provided.

We would learn more. Not long after my mom was released, my wife's dad, also in his eighties and who suffers from Parkinson's, fell and broke his hip. His wife, my mother-in-law, chose a nursing home that had the advantage of being close to where she lived. At first blush, the place looked great. The rooms were good sized and furnished rather like a mid-scale motel. The TV, in other words, wasn't screwed to the ceiling. They also served raw fruits and vegetables—a seemingly obvious nutritional thing to do that was somehow overlooked at the place my mom stayed.

The smell, though, was the same. And as weeks blurred into one another, it became clear that living conditions at dad's nursing home were pretty much the same, too—only bigger. This was a considerably larger facility with, as it turned out, a seemingly smaller staff.

So it wasn't exactly a shock when we learned over the holidays that a national study recently released by the Centers for Medicare and Medicaid Services gave the nursing home my father-in-law stayed at the lowest rating on a scale of 1 to 5. What's more, the study found that Indiana ranks among the ten worst states in the nation when it comes to quality of care. Just more than one in four of the state's nursing homes received the lowest grade possible, and about half of the five hundred facilities here were considered below average.

It's been said that Indiana doesn't take good care of its kids. Well, the situation is worse if you're old.

As we could see for ourselves, the biggest problem in nursing homes is staffing. The American Health Care Association has determined that Indiana has a mind-boggling 93 percent one-year staff turnover rate for certified nursing assistants. No wonder. At one point an aide asked my mother-in-law if she might consider hiring her to help them in their home once my father-in-law was released. When my mother-in-law said she could only pay $10 an hour, the aide said that would be great since the home only paid her $8.

Both facilities we experienced last year were for-profit. This means that necessities like raw fruits and vegetables are considered luxuries and that staff is kept to a minimum. The place my mom stayed was supposed to have a doctor, but he lived miles away and, a nurse told me, literally phoned his directions in.

It was also interesting to note how the care provided to both our parents was abruptly considered sufficient after about one hundred days—or once their Medicare coverage expired.

"Live fast, die young, and leave a good-looking corpse." Whoever said that must have come to Indiana and seen the alternative.

Blooming Algae:
Our Appetite for Freedom
June 2, 2010

"Don't look back. Something might be gaining on you," said baseball great Satchel Paige. If Mr. Paige were alive today, he might have amended his statement to say that something has its hands around our collective neck.

Exhibit A: the front page of the May 24 *Indianapolis Star* proclaiming, "What's Good for Your Grass Can Be Bad for Your Water." The story, by Jason Thomas, goes on to describe how the use of phosphorus-infused fertilizers on farms and yards and golf courses (more on those golf courses in a moment) creates runoff that acts like steroids for algae in our rivers and streams. This phosphorus-pumped algae forms enormous blooms that kill fish and affects our drinking water, making it smell and taste rotten.

A geologist from IUPUI, Lenore P. Tedesco, is quoted in the article, saying, "the vast majority of water in Indiana has an excess of phosphorus, which is causing changes in the ecosystem and creating water-quality problems."

This wasn't the first time Jason Thomas wrote about algae in our water. Just a month earlier, on April 26, he started a story titled "Algae Infusing Water With Musty Taste" with this sentence: "A naturally occurring outburst of algae in the White River is causing taste and odor issues with some Indianapolis Water customers."

The key word here is "naturally." Reassuring, isn't it? Maybe Mr. Thomas got this word from Amber Finkelstein, a spokesperson for the Indiana Department of Environmental Management. Here is Ms. Finkelstein talking about algae blooms to Channel 13:

"It is always better to let these take their course naturally, if possible, since the algae is a natural organism, allowing it to run its course and die off is likely to be less harmful than putting chemicals into the problem."

This quote comes from August 2009. Almost a year ago. Yes, putting chemicals into the problem is a problem, all right. The problem, in this case, being the White River. There is nothing natural about the amounts of phosphorus we've been allowing to run into this and other waterways for years.

Satchel Paige was right.

Something else is gaining on us—our waistlines. On Tuesday, May 25, the *Star* put this on its front page: "Our Fitness Misses the Mark." The thirty-sixth annual American College of Sports Medicine's American Fitness Index reported that Indianapolis now ranks forty-fourth out of the country's fifty most populous areas when it comes to health and fitness. Making matters worse is that we've somehow managed to drop eight places in just one year.

Obesity and smoking rates have actually gone up here in the past twelve months, as has the number of people diagnosed with diabetes. We also have fewer acres of parkland, playgrounds, and recreation centers per capita than most cities our size, and we're spending less money on our parks. Our lack of public transit is another factor, since it means a greater overall dependence on cars for commuting.

Under these circumstances, two of our strengths, according to the study, come with a heaping dose of irony. We rank high in our number of primary care givers—a seemingly classic case of supply and demand. And our metro area boasts a higher than average number of golf courses per capita. Hurray for phosphorus fertilizers! Perhaps algae will be our new state flower.

And while this news accumulates, like gouts of crude oil in a Louisiana marsh, we continue to be informed about the progress of BP's refinery expansion project in Whiting, on Indiana's Lake Michigan shore. As Elizabeth Kolbert reports in the *New Yorker*, "Having consumed most of the world's readily accessible oil, we are now compelled to look for fuel in ever more remote places, and to extract it in ever riskier and more damaging ways." BP's expansion in Indiana is intended to deal with Canadian tar sand, a dirty process that extracts the oil from a solid form, creating two to four times the amount of greenhouse gases associated with conventional oil refining. BP's Indiana project, of course, is touted for the jobs it will create. Perhaps some of the newly unemployed along the Gulf Coast will consider migrating here.

This is turning into a season of blame. Blame BP or the government for a lack of damage control in the Gulf. Blame the makers of fast and highly processed food for trans fats and empty calories. Blame fertilizers for turning our waterways into blooming algae gardens.

Ultimately, though, the blame bounces back to you and me. Our appetites have created this situation, become so consuming that we've come to confuse them with freedom itself. We could quit using phosphorus in favor of other, more earth-friendly fertilizers; we could make unhealthy foods more expensive; we could commit ourselves to reinventing society around safer, more sustainable forms of energy. But we don't because, in every case, it would mean intruding on someone's idea of what it means to be free.

"Don't look back," said Satchel Paige. Today he'd be telling us to look in the mirror.

BP Is Indiana's Problem, Too: A Big Polluter on the Lake
May 12, 2010

A week ago I was in Florida, where the ever-widening oil slick in the Gulf of Mexico was local news. People there were bracing for a calamity, the likes of which they had never dared imagine. On the Gulf side, they feared losing their fishing and tourism industries.

And there was concern that if the oil drifted to the south, it might be picked up by currents below Florida's southern tip and start washing up on beaches on the state's eastern coast as well.

It's safe to say that no one in the oil industry saw this coming. There had been disastrous oil spills, but they occurred as oil was being carried from one place to another. A deep-sea rupture at the source, where oil was being extracted, was—we were told—practically unheard of.

Offshore oil drilling was considered to be so failsafe that even President Obama felt secure in calling for more of it, reversing his stated position on the issue in order to try and woo congressional support for climate legislation.

Messing with oil seemed like a relatively innocuous thing to do. Until, that is, oil started messing with us.

It figured that the oil company at the root of the Gulf gusher would be British-based oil giant BP. As Jason Leopold's excellent reporting for the online digest *Truthout* has shown, BP has been on the wrong end of a litany of safety violations going back almost a decade.

There was a fine levied against a BP drilling rig in 2003 for "failure to follow the procedures established in the Job Safety Analysis (JSA)"; in 2004 another BP rig was cited because a "diverted system was not installed as in the approved plan…leading to damage to property and the environment." In 2005 an explosion at BP's Texas refinery killed 15 people and injured 170. BP was fined $50 million for that incident and pleaded guilty to a felony. In 2006 two oil spills in Alaska's Prudhoe Bay resulted in a $20 million fine and another guilty plea to a criminal violation of the Clean Water Act.

Leopold writes, "The issues related to the repeated spills in Prudhoe Bay and elsewhere were revealed by more than 100 whistleblowers who, since as far back as 1999, said the company failed to take seriously their warnings about shoddy safety practices and instead retaliated against whistleblowers who registered complaints with superiors."

It was in the midst of all this that Governor Mitch Daniels

stood up with BP America's Chairman and President Bob Malone in 2006 to announce the proposed expansion of BP's Whiting refinery on Lake Michigan. "We appreciate BP's choice of Indiana for this massive, landmark project…The eyes of the whole state are on Northwest Indiana today, as they should be. This marks another huge step in Indiana's economic comeback."

The expansion was being undertaken in advance of BP's plan to begin refining heavy crude oil from the tar sands in Alberta, Canada. Tar sands oil is particularly dirty, and the refining process emits a large volume of greenhouse gases.

In 2007 BP asked Daniels and Thomas Easterly, head of Indiana's Department of Environmental Management, for permission to increase the amount of toxic waste it flushed into the lake. Not long after that, IDEM granted BP an exemption from federal regulations regarding air pollution because BP claimed halving the amount of particulates the refinery emits would not be economically feasible.

The Whiting refinery expansion and its fallout raised howls of protest from environmentalists in northwest Indiana and from elected officials along the Lake Michigan coast in Illinois, Wisconsin, and Michigan. Protests forced BP to temporarily back off its Lake Michigan dumping plans, but the soot it is putting in the air remains an issue. In mid-April, less than a week before the Gulf crisis began, a group of concerned BP shareholders went so far as to propose that BP review risks related to tar sand oil, but that proposal was voted down.

"The resolution failed so it'll have no impact on the project," said a BP spokesperson. "We factored the price of carbon into our projects and Whiting is no exception. The project continues to move forward. We'll have 3,000 on the job this year working on the project." The refinery expansion is due for completion in 2011.

As far as BP is concerned, the potential profits from tar sand oil outweigh the costs of pollution. As far as the Daniels administration is concerned, those three thousand jobs do, too. Daniels and Easterly have adamantly rejected environmental concerns about the Whiting expansion, insisting there's nothing to worry about and that BP is a solid corporate partner. They insist the project's advantages outweigh any risks.

If all this sounds terribly familiar, it should. Once again BP is at the center of a risky practice involving extracting, transporting, and refining oil. Once again, we hear confident voices assuring us that the bottom line is what matters. The difference is that this BP story is taking place here, in our own backyard. To paraphrase the governor, if the eyes of the entire state aren't on what BP is doing in northwest Indiana, they should be.

A Twenty-First Century Catch-22: Affirmative Action at IUPUI
February 27, 2008

Keith John Sampson never thought he could get in trouble for reading a book, let alone on a college campus, but that's what happened. Sampson is a man in his early fifties. He does janitorial work for the campus facility services at IUPUI, where he's been gradually accumulating the credits for a degree in communications studies. He has ten credit hours to go.

"Being on that campus has really been an experience for me," Sampson told me not long ago. It's an experience that got a lot more complicated last year.

Sampson is an avid reader. It's been his habit to bring books to work with him, so that he can read in the break room when he's not on the clock. Last year, Sampson was working in IUPUI's Medical Science Building. It turns out the break room there is across from the morgue, which, as Sampson pointed out to me, is kind of ironic when you stop to think about it.

At the time, Sampson was reading a book he had checked out from the public library. That book, *Notre Dame vs. the Klan: How the Fighting Irish Defeated the Ku Klux Klan*, features a slightly grainy black and white photograph of the University of Notre Dame's famous golden dome on the cover. Its author is Todd Tucker, a professional writer and Notre Dame grad; the publisher is Loyola Press of Loyola University in Chicago.

The book is about how for two days in May 1924, a group of Notre Dame students got into a street fight with members of the Ku Klux Klan. The Klan was meeting in South Bend for the express purpose of attacking Catholicism and sticking a collective thumb in the eye of the country's most famous Catholic university. The book was a *Notre Dame Magazine* "Pick of the Week" and garnered an average customer review of 4.5 stars on Amazon.com. In its review, the *Indiana Magazine of History* noted that Tucker "succeeds in placing the event in a broad framework that includes the origins and development of both the Klan and Notre Dame."

Sampson recalls that his AFSCME shop steward noticed him reading the book and told him that reading a book about the Klan was like bringing pornography to work. He wasn't interested in hearing what the book was actually about. Another time, a co-worker who was sitting across the table from Sampson in the break room commented that she found the Klan offensive. Sampson says that when he tried to explain the book, she said she wasn't interested in talking about it, either.

A few weeks passed. Then Sampson got a message ordering him to report to Marguerite Watkins at the IUPUI Affirmative Action Office. He was told a co-worker had filed a racial harassment complaint against him for reading *Notre Dame vs. the Klan*. Sampson says he tried to explain to Ms. Watkins that he had gotten the book from the public library, and that it was a story about how students stood up to the Klan. He says he tried to show her the book, but that Ms. Watkins had no interest in seeing it.

Then Sampson received a letter, dated Nov. 25, 2007, from

Lillian Charleston of IUPUI's Affirmative Action Office. The letter begins by saying that the AAO has completed its investigation of a co-worker's allegation that Sampson "racially harassed her by repeatedly reading the book, *Notre Dame vs. the Klan: How the Fighting Irish Defeated the Ku Klux Klan* by Todd Tucker in the presence of Black employees." It goes on to say, "you demonstrated disdain and insensitivity to your co-workers who repeatedly requested that you refrain from reading the book which has such an inflammatory and offensive topic in their presence...you used extremely poor judgment by insisting on openly reading the book related to a historically and racially abhorrent subject in the presence of your Black co-workers." Charleston went on to say that according to "the legal 'reasonable person standard,' a majority of adults are aware of and understand how repugnant the KKK is to African Americans..."

Sampson was ordered to stop reading the book in the immediate presence of his co-workers and, when reading the book, to sit apart from them.

"I feel like I've been caught up in a twenty-first-century version of Catch-22," says Sampson, who has never been given the opportunity to officially face any of his accusers, let alone try to tell them that *Notre Dame vs. the Klan* isn't even about African Americans. When I tried calling the Affirmative Action Office, I was told their policy was to never speak to the media.

But, says Sampson, this episode could be an opportunity. He would welcome the chance to participate in a moderated forum that might use his experience as an entry point for a larger discussion dealing with intellectual freedom on the IUPUI campus.

That's a good idea. For Sampson's sake, I hope ideas still count at IUPUI.

Carmel's Palladium:
An Unabashed Throwback
July 7, 2010

By now I'm sure you've seen the television ads for the Center for the Performing Arts, in Carmel. They feature a wash of pastel colors and an artist's rendering of the Center's signature venue, the Palladium.

The Palladium is just one of four performance spaces at the center. There are also a five-hundred-seat proscenium theater, a two-hundred-seat studio theater, and an outdoor amphitheater.

But the Palladium is the trademark. Based on a villa designed by Renaissance architect Andrea Palladio near Vicenza, in Italy, the Palladium is an unabashed throwback. Its limestone dome rises up from what once was a farmer's field like a Viennese fantasy concocted on a backlot at MGM during the 1930s. The sight of the place conjures images of women in bustled gowns and men in top hats, of carriages and brass-tipped canes.

In creating this old world setting, the good people of Carmel are seemingly flying in the face of contemporary cultural trends. Nowadays, the vast majority of our cultural institutions are practically falling over themselves with populist fervor, doing all they can to seem as easy going and down home as a corner bar or shopping mall.

It used to be that cultural institutions were about uplift and aspiration. We dressed up to go to the symphony or museum, where we were introduced to achievements that stood for the best that human beings were capable of.

In the very act of putting on our best clothes for these experiences, struggling unsuccessfully with that tie or wiping the dust off dress shoes that were a size too small, we momentarily stepped out of our everyday selves in preparation for something we might not understand but were advised would be extraordinary.

Well, all of this fell to pieces like the pages of an old paperback copy of *Pride and Prejudice*. A generation raised on rock concerts and theme parks spread the news that going to museums or concert halls was for stiffs. And as the administrators responsible for attracting people saw their clientele dwindling and, worse, aging, they began trying to make themselves over in order to be more cool, or hip, or whatever it was that drew crowds.

So orchestras began playing movie themes and serving cocktails. Museums opened ever-larger gift shops. Everybody invested in lasers and digital projection units. As for dressing up, forget it.

Today, the people found in cultural venues dress the same as they do at airports—another experience, by the way, that's been culturally downsized. For the most part, they dress like big-bodied children.

Let's face it: we Americans, regardless of income level or education, have never gotten the hang of casual dress. From back alleys to country clubs, we either turn ourselves into walking advertisements for tourist traps and fashion brands, with logos, legends, and dopey one-liners scrawled across our tops and bottoms, or else, taking our cues from *Vicarious Living Magazine,* we adopt the looks of professional athletes and rock stars when, in fact, few of us have the money, the bodies, or the energy to pull this off.

Men are particularly clueless. If America is such a land of opportunity, why is it so many American men insist on dressing like adolescents? There was a time when most kids couldn't wait to grow up—that's where all the good stuff was waiting. Now, apparently, the future is so bleak, young men present themselves as though they're trying to prolong their teen years as long as possible.

Somewhere along the line, the idea got around that there was something confining about dressing thoughtfully. It was considered to be a sign of conformity that went with a buttoned-up corporate job and an inhibited way of life. It meant that you cared too much about what other people thought, that you were uptight.

The same went for the places we used to associate with dressing up. As people came to present themselves more casually, they also began to take museums and concert halls less seriously. Now if we are mystified or bored by what we find in these places, it's the fault of the art being offered. The idea of taking the time to acquire a taste for something has become as old-fashioned as a Homburg hat.

Our dressed-down approach to culture reflects our political attitudes. While having a truly smart guy as president seems a good thing in theory, it appears most of us are put off by this in practice. Better to have someone as pissed off by what goes on in the world as we are. That's leadership!

So I am delighted by Carmel's decision to create a cultural venue that evokes a more rarefied world. It's a bold move that promises nothing less than a recasting of our cultural expectations. Although I doubt the Palladium will require people to dress a certain way, its design constitutes a kind of dress code in itself. The first person to walk in there wearing a t-shirt or ball cap is bound to feel a little weird, like they've stepped back in time.

Then, as scheduled to perform in January, Neil Sedaka will take the stage, and the effect will be complete.

The Arts, or Else!
Butler University's Culture Credit
August 11, 2010

Butler University announced last week that, beginning with this year's freshman class, all students will be required to attend one cultural event per semester. Members of Butler's Class of 2014 will attend eight performances or extracurricular lectures during the course of their college careers.

It used to be that studying abroad for a time was the standard way for a college student to broaden her horizon. Indeed, Butler still has an extensive program for students who want the experience of being for a time in another country.

Now, apparently, the arts are another country. Butler students will, in effect, need to get their cultural passports stamped a certain number of times if they want a diploma.

The administrators at Butler should be congratulated for recognizing that a college education should include dimensions that reach beyond the classroom. College isn't just a place, but a time when individuals can take their first steps outside the circles of family, their childhood, and received ideas and beliefs. Life-changing experiences are liable to happen here. And it's entirely possible that, given the opportunity, some of those experiences might involve watching the movement of bodies in a dance, feeling the emotional impact of a play, or hearing the way sounds are arranged in an experimental piece of music.

If there is a whiff of melancholy in Butler's decision, it's that such a requirement is considered necessary. Colleges are their own, self-regarding communities. That's why, for generations, students have referred to life outside the campus as "the real world." Given a community where art is being created by one's peers in multiple places on an almost daily basis, you'd think that students would come to find attending arts offerings to be as natural as sharing a meal with friends.

But when it comes to the arts, it seems that even a relatively small campus like Butler's, 4,500 students, is getting more like that other, supposedly more "real," world outside. A world, that is, where even so-called educated people think of the arts as being for someone else.

It's no secret that traditional arts organizations today are fighting harder than ever for each soul they can cajole through the door. Last year, a study released by the National Endowment for the Arts found attendance down for practically every form of art in every type of venue. While it was tempting to blame the sick economy for this slippage, the NEA study was unforgiving: it showed a trend line that extended back for years, including economic booms as well as busts.

Tellingly, the only indisputable area of arts audience growth has been online. People have increasingly been turning to their computers to look at types of performance that have always been defined as "live," muddling William Butler Yeats' question, "How can we know the dancer from the dance?" more than he could possibly have guessed.

It is impossible not to see a connection between this situation and the general erosion of what are called the liberal arts on most college campuses. As the cost of a college education has climbed up beyond the stratosphere, staggering many household incomes and driving a large percentage of graduates into levels of debt that all but foreclose on their choice of careers, college has become less about learning how to learn through life experience and more about training for a place in the corporate hierarchy.

Humanities majors such as English, philosophy, and history see declining enrollments and cuts to programs as students and their parents feel a greater and greater need to justify the outlandish cost of college with a professional payoff upon graduation.

Under these circumstances, it's not surprising that, for many students, the arts seem either extraneous to their ambitions or else are judged almost entirely in terms of their occasional ability to provide escapist relief from the competitive pressure to turn college's financial shock therapy into a moneymaking proposition.

For these students, college as a place for lifetime firsts has been reduced to the first step in the rat race. It's no wonder that, having had little or no meaningful experience with the arts, so many college grads are oblivious to what the arts have to offer. That they turn out to be just as ill-equipped to find creative, sustainable solutions for our collective healthcare, environmental, energy, and employment woes is probably more than a coincidence.

It's possible that some students at Butler will see the new requirement to attend arts events as the equivalent of a charm school exercise, like learning which fork to use with salad. But firsthand experience with the arts should provide the students with more than a flush of social embellishment. The arts, ultimately, are languages suggesting ways to join our heads and hearts. In form and function they provide the opportunity for experiences that show us new ways of thinking, feeling, being. As Kurt Vonnegut liked to say, they make your soul grow.

Let's hope one event per semester is enough.

Half Empty or Half Full: A False Choice
February 28, 2012

Is the glass half full or half empty? That's the question we were asked to consider last week as first President Obama and then Governor Daniels presented their contrasting views of the economy.

In his annual State of the Union address, the president described what he called "the American promise" this way: "If you worked hard, you could do well enough to raise a family, own a home, send your kids to college, and put a little away for retirement." He then said that, "the defining issue of our time is how to keep that promise alive."

As far as the president is concerned, the glass appears to be half full. In the last twenty-two months, he said, businesses have created more than three million jobs. That's the most jobs created in a year since 2005. He went on to say that American manufacturers are adding jobs for the first time since the 1990s.

But Governor Daniels, who gave the Republican response following the president's speech, had a different take. For him, the glass is half empty. "The percentage of Americans with jobs is at the lowest in decades," he said. "One of five men of prime working age, and nearly half of all persons under thirty, did not go to work today."

The governor sounded the alarm. This year, he said, may be our last chance "to restore an America of hope and upward mobility, and greater equality." He said the US is "only a short distance behind Greece, Spain, and other European countries now facing economic catastrophe."

Like President Obama, Governor Daniels asserted that creating jobs is the way back to "an America of promise." But he accused the president of putting business down. "The late Steve Jobs—what a fitting name he had—created more of them than all those stimulus dollars the president borrowed and blew. Out here, in Indiana, when a businessperson asks me what he can do for our state, I say 'First, make money. Be successful.'"

As far as Governor Daniels is concerned, the president's faith in government is misplaced; it's American business know-how that will see us through. To hear him tell it, the governor's calendar is packed with meetings in which eager business executives are pushing in front of one another to ask what they can do for Indiana—besides make financial contributions to local Republican candidates, that is.

The governor alluded to Steve Jobs. But in an eye-opening piece in the January 22 *New York Times*, reporters Charles Duhigg and Keith Bradsher write about how the economies of manufacturing have prompted Apple to outsource engineering, building, and assembly of iPads and iPhones to overseas contractors. Apple employs 43,000 people in the US but pays 700,000 people in Asia, Europe, and elsewhere. A former Apple executive is quoted as saying Apple's entire supply chain is now in China.

The iPhone is assembled at a place called Foxconn City, where 230,000 employees live in barracks and are paid $17 per day to work six twelve-hour days per week. Duhigg and Bradsher note that the Chinese government has, in many cases, underwritten the costs of numerous industries in their country, such as the building of worker dormitories.

Given his support for union-busting right-to-work legislation, this story makes you wonder what Governor Daniels had in mind when he linked Steve Jobs and job creation.

It's worth noting that Indiana already has its own version of the Chinese production model. For years, farms and orchards with a need for seasonal labor have hired Hispanic workers to come here and harvest fruits and vegetables. These workers often work from dawn to dusk. They also live in barracks or bunkhouses. The farmers who hire them will often tell you they've tried to employ local folks, but most Americans either can't or won't do the work as well as their migrant competition. At least, not for that pay scale.

Both Governor Daniels and President Obama seem to agree that America has a jobs problem. But the jobs problem is actually a competition problem. If the terms of this competition are left to business leaders to decide on their own, the issue will be reduced, as it seems to be in Indiana, to figuring out how to get the most out of workers for the least amount of money.

This is why the president is proposing to create tax incentives, making it more attractive for businesses to stay in this country. Whether these measures are sufficient, though, remains to be seen.

Duhigg and Bradsher write that American business leaders complain our workers lack mid-level skills and that the cost of doing business here is just too high to allow for the profits necessary to spur innovation. What's more, as economist Betsey Stevenson tells them, "Companies once felt an obligation to support American workers… That's disappeared."

So is the glass half empty, or half full? Maybe, when it comes to our economic dilemma, it's time to stop thinking in such either/or terms. Neither government nor business can fix things by itself.

Why Is Lugar Smiling?:
Loyalty Has a Price
April 27, 2005

The past couple of weeks have not been easy for Richard Lugar. Indiana's seventy-two-year-old senator-for-life is the chairman of the prestigious Senate Foreign Relations Committee. In that capacity, it has been Lugar's job to shepherd President George Bush's nominee for ambassador to the United Nations, John Bolton, through the confirmation process.

This should not have been a problem. Republicans outnumber Democrats on the committee by 10–8. And, at least here in Indiana, Lugar has a reputation for being a sage conciliator. One would have thought that he was the perfect guy to massage away the kinks created by Bolton's rash of past utterances about the institution the president has chosen him to serve. Things like: "The [United Nations] secretariat building in New York has thirty-eight stories. If you lost ten stories today it wouldn't make a bit of difference."

What's more, although the folks here in Indiana like to see Lugar as an independent thinker, a man of integrity who can't be bought, he is, in fact, nothing if not a good soldier for his party and his party's president.

Over the years Lugar has managed to win support from moderates and even some liberals thanks to a personal style that manages to express a seemingly thoughtful concern about issues from, say, drilling for oil in the Alaskan Wildlife Refuge to going to war in Iraq. No sooner do the potentates in his party express their latest radical scheme than St. Richard appears in public to soften the rhetoric and put a seemingly rational spin on things.

Reporters then fall all over themselves speculating that, perhaps, Lugar is actually opposing Bush, Inc. They did this before the last election when Lugar called Iraq reconstruction efforts "incompetent." They did it again two weeks ago when Lugar opened the

Bolton hearings by scolding Mr. Bolton for his penchant for self-expression, saying, "In the diplomatic world, neither bluntness nor rhetorical sensitivity is a virtue in itself."

But after Lugar expresses his reservations about the world according to George W. Bush, he invariably winds up doing whatever the president wants. *Congressional Quarterly* rates him Bush's biggest fan in the Senate at 99.2 percent. He has voted with Bush 251 times in 253 chances. No wonder the *National Journal* ranks him among the Senate's most conservative members.

So Lugar's high school principal-like performance following the testimony of Carl Ford, the retired chief of the State Department's Bureau of Intelligence and Research (INR) was chilling, but not surprising. Ford, a lifelong Republican, came forward two weeks ago to testify against Bolton. This was televised on C-Span. It was clear that Ford, despite his loyalty to his party, has a conscience that has been grievously insulted by Bolton. He felt a need to speak out and share his professional assessment of this guy. In essence, Ford said that Bolton went further than any political appointee he had ever seen to try and twist intelligence to fit the White House agenda.

Ford put himself on the line to tell this story. When he was done, Richard Lugar smiled. Lugar kept smiling as he went on to say that Ford's story was interesting but that it didn't matter. Bolton, Lugar said, was the president's choice. He was Secretary of State Rice's choice. They were entitled to their choice and, whatever Bolton had done in the past, Lugar was sure he'd behave himself henceforth and not do or say anything without permission from his betters. He said he looked forward to Bolton's confirmation. The sweat was still shining on Ford's brow, but he made a point of going up and shaking Lugar's hand anyway.

Much has been made of Bolton's abusive management style. This has obscured a larger point. Leading up to the Iraq war, Ford's INR was right in its intelligence assessments about Iraq when the CIA was wrong. The INR downplayed Saddam's firepower and predicted a difficult postwar transition. But the INR was ignored and ostracized because what it said didn't fit the White House plan. Bolton was a White House enforcer. Now the White House wants to put him on the world stage at the United Nations, where he will probably be called on to present the US case for policy having to do with countries like Iran and North Korea. Given his record—and after what happened to Colin Powell—will anyone, friend or foe, believe him?

Last week, Richard Lugar was smiling again, but things were not going according to plan. George Voinovich, the Republican senator from Ohio, was behaving the way Hoosiers like to think Lugar behaves, actually acting on principle and saying that what he heard about Bolton troubled him and that he thought more investigation was warranted. Lugar was vexed, but he had to go along—the votes for Bolton were disappearing.

As I watched our senior senator's forced smile, I wondered what frustrated him more, this runaway process, or that his commander-in-chief had stuck him with having to promote such a flawed and dismal candidate. All those votes. That unwavering support. And Richard Lugar is left dusting John Bolton's shoulders and holding his bag. The price of loyalty is high indeed.

High School Is Boring: So What?
June 9, 2010

About half our kids find school boring.

This news flash comes courtesy of an annual study conducted by the Indiana University Center for Postsecondary Research. Every year, researchers ask tens of thousands of high school students to share their "thoughts, beliefs, and perceptions" about school. The 2009 survey covered 103 schools in twenty-seven states.

According to a press release distributed by IU, the numbers between 2006 and 2009 have consistently shown what's called a "troubling trend."

A lot of kids find school boring.

"About 49 percent of the kids are bored every day, 17 percent every class," says Ethan Yazzie-Mintz, the survey's project director.

Among some of the 2009 survey's other findings: 41 percent of students say they went to school because of what they learn in classes; 23 percent said they went because of their teachers; about a third said they went because they actually enjoyed being in school.

It's been a long time since I went to high school, but I have to say that, based on my experience, these numbers aren't that surprising. Boredom was part of what going to school was all about. In this, going to school was, in fact, preparation for life in the working world. We can't all be undersea explorers or bomb disposal specialists. Coping with boredom—indeed, rising above it—is something most people have to be able to do for a large share of their working lives. School was a useful preview.

Only 2 percent of the students surveyed said they were never bored in school. These kids were either obsessive-compulsive brown-nosers, or they don't have lives, which roughly amounts to the same thing.

I would say that 41 percent of the kids saying they went to school because of their classes is actually pretty good. There's a lot of learning that takes place in high school that has nothing to do with academics. One reason I went to high school was to meet girls. Another was to hang out with my friends. Although I was, on a couple of occasions, required to report to the principal about ensuing misadventures with my fellow classmates, I was never tested on these subjects. That was good; their effects were incalculable.

An off-putting aspect of the survey is its tendency to make school sound like a retail proposition. I didn't go to school because that was the way I wanted to spend my days. I went because I had to. My parents wouldn't have it any other way.

Parents are never mentioned in the survey findings released by

IU. The press release makes it seem as if school is just one of many options kids have (which, given increasingly high drop-out rates, is turning out to be true in too many cases). Therefore it's up to schools to find ways to make themselves more attractive, to compete for kids' attention. Or, in the words of the survey, enhance "student engagement."

But the basis of student engagement begins at home. Parents provide the sense of purpose necessary to enable a kid to make it through the frustration and, yes, boredom, of diagramming sentences and algebra. Without this parental bedrock, kids are on their own, left to make what pass for decisions based on little more than an appetite for consumption.

Disconnects between parents and kids are why so many efforts at school reform—attempts, that is, to compensate for dysfunctional parenting—don't work. From voucher experiments and charter schools to a quadrupling of per-pupil spending in the United States between 1960 and 2005, nothing has been proven to consistently improve student performance. The refrain that our schools are failing, accompanied by chest-thumping percussion courtesy of the state and national poo-bahs charged with turning things around, has become a kind of national elevator music.

Yazzie-Mintz says, "Many students would be more engaged in school if they were intellectually challenged by their work." He cites discussion and debate as two effective forms of teaching, adding that technology projects, art, and drama projects also score high on kids' lists of things to do.

But then we've known these things for generations. Art and drama projects helped rescue my high school experience. But these are the types of programs that are being cut as school curriculums are squeezed and test scores are made the be-all and end-all of how we evaluate our schools and the people who teach.

Schools aren't substitutes for conscientious parenting. Nor can they expect to lay a full and dynamic claim to the attention of the sleep-deprived, hormone-busting kids who walk through their doors.

The trouble is that in all our attempts at reforming systems, we have never come to grips with what an education should be. Is it job training? Or a more general preparation for handling the slings, arrows—and boring patches—of citizenship in an unpredictable world? Until we reach a working agreement about this, our schools will be worse than boring. They'll be pointless.

Language on Display at the IMA: Talking to Ourselves
April 1, 2009

The opening weekend for the Indianapolis Museum of Art's marquee show, *European Design Since 1985: Shaping the New Century*, took place a month ago, but something I observed there has stuck with me like lint on a black jacket.

The IMA hosted a symposium featuring a who's who of European design stars. They came from such countries as France, Spain, Sweden, Belgium, Switzerland, Italy, Germany, and the Netherlands. Over the course of two days, many of these guests were asked to make a thirty-minute presentation and then to answer questions as part of a panel.

Here is what knocked me out: Almost all of these people were more or less able to speak English. Many spoke it well enough to be funny (on purpose).

They made it easy for the American audience to feel cosmopolitan. It didn't matter whether a particular speaker hailed from Stockholm or Milan, we understood her just the same. It was tempting to sit back and reflect, Disney-style, that it's a small world after all.

But it was practically impossible for me to imagine myself in any of the presenters' stylish shoes. If a museum in Berlin, say, or Paris invited me to talk for thirty minutes about anything, all I'd be able to say would be "hello" and "good-bye." Even if someone wrote a speech for me in the appropriate language, I'd probably make "head of state" sound like "knucklehead."

I found myself thinking that their multilingualism might be a key to why Europeans are different from Americans and, in particular, how it is they seem to be cleaning our clocks now when it comes to cutting edge creativity.

My guess was that most of the presenters at the IMA not only spoke English; they probably had a better than passing ability to make themselves understood in the tongues of one or more of their European neighbors, as well.

Technology may have all but eliminated old-fashioned geographical provincialism. Anyone, no matter where they live, can use Google to see the latest works by artists and designers from anywhere in the world with a few keystrokes.

But creative enterprise is also a highly social form of interaction in which the communication of ideas serves as fuel. The ability to communicate across a range of languages is as important a part of the artist's toolkit as it is the diplomat's.

The contemporary art scene today is nothing if not global. Creative people who want their work to matter in more than a strictly local sense are obligated to be aware and prepared to address developments wherever they occur.

No one, obviously, can speak every language. But the ability to be a citizen of the world almost certainly involves being able to at least navigate with minimal competence in more than one. A facility with languages seems to increase not just verbal vocabulary, but a larger vocabulary of options when it comes to the kinds of problem solving that all creative people are confronted with everyday.

Americans have had it easy. We have taken cover and comfort in the notion that the language we speak is omni-national, the language of business, of power. The Web may be worldwide, but English is its dominant language. Walk into a three-star restaurant anywhere across the globe and try ordering a meal in the local tongue; chances are your waiter will reply in English and save you, in the process, from getting liver when you thought you were asking for fish.

Too many of us have even gone so far as to take umbrage, when visiting Paris, say, at the natives' occasional unwillingness to regard our linguistic ineptitude as anything other than what it actually is: a fundamental lack of respect.

Nothing betrays our imperial attitude more convincingly than our seemingly abiding conviction that the rest of the world owes it to itself to learn English. Or else.

The problem with this mindset is that it isolates us at exactly the time when we need to be finding ways to connect with other countries and cultures. We can thump our chests all we want about how productive and innovative we are, but the evidence suggests otherwise. Whether it's our inability to design cars that combine fuel efficiency with genuine style, or the increasing numbers of people who go abroad for medical procedures that are unaffordable at home, we are slipping.

Our carelessness when it comes to learning other people's languages suggests a society more absorbed in talking to itself than to its neighbors. This puts us at a real disadvantage, but it's not insurmountable. Europe, after all, had to live through one punishing war after another before arriving at today's productive, albeit still tenuous, union.

"Bad artists copy," said Picasso. "Great artists steal." There are plenty of ideas worth stealing embedded in the IMA's *European Design* show. But if I were to pick just one, it would have to do with how our world is made by the languages we allow ourselves to speak.

Jim Irsay Is Right: Reality Bites
May 6, 2009

You know you're in trouble when Jim Irsay looks like the only adult in the room.

That's the way it seems at this point in the city's continuing battle with reality also known as the CIB debacle. The CIB, or Capital Improvement Board, is the politically appointed board of insiders who use tax dollars to run projects that Indianapolis' Business Party deems too important to put up for a public vote.

Did you vote to make Indianapolis a Sports Capital? To blow up Market Square Arena? Can you remember seeing a ballot with a box on it where you were asked to check whether or not you thought building a new football stadium (with retractable dome) was a good idea? I didn't think so.

Voting can be a messy, unpredictable business. Ex-Mayor Bart Peterson will vouch for that. When the Business Party decides it wants something, it knows better than to leave the process up to mugs like you and me. It relies on the CIB.

This is called efficiency.

You might think of the CIB as the Business Party's enabler. The problem with enablers is that they sometimes help perpetuate bad habits. They don't know how to say "no."

And so today the CIB finds itself in charge of a basketball arena and a football stadium that seemed like good ideas at the time, but that it doesn't know how to pay for.

The CIB needs $47.5 million.

The process of trying to come up with a formula for this amount heated up in January, with the beginning of the state legislative session. The hope in Indianapolis was that legislators would allow the city to keep certain types of revenue that would ordinarily go to the state, while permitting the city to jigger its tax rates on things like alcohol.

Oh, and politicians at both state and local levels got the bright idea that the teams using those stadiums—the Colts and Pacers—should kick in $5 million each to help the CIB.

This seemed reasonable. The Pacers, after all, pay chronic bad boy Jamaal Tinsley close to $7 million a year just to stay away, and the Colts reportedly saved another $7 million when they let Marvin Harrison go. What's a mere $5 million between friends?

At the Statehouse, Senator Luke Kenley from Noblesville drafted a potential funding package to bail out the CIB. It relied on both sports teams contributing $5 million each. Not to be outdone, current Mayor Greg Ballard came forth with a plan; it also included $5 million contributions from "our" Colts and Pacers.

A chorus of editorials and commentaries appeared in local media calling on the Colts and Pacers to be good corporate citizens.

The only problem was that no one, apparently, talked to the team owners—Jim Irsay of the Colts and the Pacers' Simon brothers.

Jim Irsay finally pulled the plug on these schemes. He told the Associated Press his team had already contributed $100 million to the stadium project and that a deal was a deal: his team signed a thirty-year contract with the city, and he had no intention of renegotiating it.

Such candor was bracing, if very un-Hoosier.

Typically PR-obsessed moguls don't generally court unpopularity this way, but Irsay did it. And what was the public response? Not outrage, but a kind of collective, tail-tucking gulp.

By calling the $5 million request tantamount to a renegotiation, Irsay served notice about a couple of things. First, that this could be a slippery slope. So we bail out the CIB this year; what's to keep them from going back in the hole? There still appears to be no viable plan for keeping up with the cost of maintaining the Luc.

But Irsay's calling the request for cash a renegotiation also implied a kind of Pandora's Box effect. What if Los Angeles came calling? The Colts got a great deal from Indianapolis, but the new stadium's been open less than a year and here we are, asking for another $5 million. Where does this end, in another city?

Renegotiating contracts—or just breaking them—is standard NFL operating procedure. Marvin Harrison was signed through 2010. But he lost a step. Adios, Marvin.

The business relationship between the Colts and Indianapolis is more complicated and more binding but, whether he intended it or not, Irsay put the city on notice. You want to renegotiate our deal? Be careful what you wish for.

Suddenly, the city's vaunted sports strategy was face-to-face with a new reality. The Colts represent the National Football League, one of corporate America's most powerful combines. Proximity to this corporate power is why we've wanted an NFL presence here. But this is also a power that dwarfs our resources and, when necessary, is prepared to bluntly remind us how lucky (and small) we really are.

This was the grown-up message that Jim Irsay delivered to the ditherers that insist that Indianapolis can live beyond its means. I think we should thank him.

Peyton Manning—Champion: This Doesn't Happen Very Often
February 8, 2012

He grew up in New Orleans and came of age in Tennessee. Who would have guessed that Peyton Manning had so much Hoosier in him?

If ever there was proof for the contention that Indianapolis is America's northernmost southern city, this may be it. Manning (most of us call him Peyton) made this his adopted home in less time than it takes most newcomers to find Meridian Street.

There's an undeniably weird alchemy that can take place between a truly great athlete and the town where he or she lives. At a certain point, it becomes clear that the athlete is not only playing for a team, helping it to win but, in some way, is also representing the larger community.

It's easy, even justifiable, to put down the fan's tendency to over-identify with their favorite team: to say "we" instead of "they" when talking about the outcome of a game or a coaching decision that, in fact, is completely beyond the fan's control or ken.

But something different happens when a true champion comes along. The champion actually raises everybody's game a little, even if only on a subliminal level. This doesn't happen very often—maybe once in a generation, if you're lucky.

Peyton Manning has been that kind of champion for Indianapolis. In an era when most quarterbacks are nothing more than game managers, executing plays sent to them from coaches sitting in skyboxes, Peyton has called his own games at the line of scrimmage. In this, he most resembles the leader of a great jazz band. There is art in what Peyton does. It hasn't always worked the way he wanted it to; sometimes his vision exceeds his grasp. But a Colts game featuring Peyton Manning under center has never been anything less than an experiment in mastery.

Peyton Manning, in other words, has provided this otherwise arts-skeptical city with what I would call an aesthetic experience on every weekend of football season for over a decade. When you think about all the people—not just football fans, either—in Indianapolis who have had the chance, at one time or another, to have experienced this…well, it's hard not to think that, somehow, a little bit of that mastery has rubbed off.

That should be enough to explain Peyton's place in this city, but there's more. The guy's made us laugh. No athlete in memory has been such a viral media presence. Peyton's pitilessly dry, self-depre-cating sense of humor expressed through scads of TV commercials and, memorably, on *Saturday Night Live*, has always felt just right, fitting comfortably in a line of descent starting with Kin Hubbard and including Kurt Vonnegut (another Peyton fan, by the way) and David Letterman.

Then there's the charity work, starting with purchasing athletic gear for local public high schools and culminating in a major contribution to the St. Vincent's children's hospital bearing his name.

And did I mention a certain stadium? Now that we're rubbing the Super Bowl pixie dust from our eyes, we might recall that without Peyton, without the way he elevated a previously hapless team, there would have been scant support for a publicly funded downtown football stadium. It's an indication of just how corporate the economics of pro sports have become that money, not local history, determined the naming of this massive landmark. It should be named what people call it: The House that Peyton Built.

Peyton himself, of course, is part of this corporate culture. He's been lavishly—some would say obscenely—rewarded for the way he plays what is, finally, a game.

Corporate culture has a momentum of its own. Local stories, memories, and sentimental affections are rarely able to stand up to the force that gathers at the bottom line. So for all Peyton Manning has meant to Indianapolis, the story he has created here appears to be coming to an end, hastened unceremoniously by injury. The financial calculus that made Peyton ridiculously rich now makes it impossible to take a chance on keeping him around.

My son calls me from his home in North Carolina where, every day, he follows the news about Peyton on the Internet and via sports talk radio. He is a man now, but when Peyton started playing for the Colts, my son wasn't even old enough to have a driver's license. He wants to talk about what's happening, and I hear resignation and regret in his voice.

He knows the Colts will likely draft a new quarterback, the aptly named Andrew Luck. He understands this means the odds are Peyton Manning will never play another game in an Indianapolis uniform. For my son I sense that this is not only the end of an era— it's the end of a certain relationship he's had with his hometown. Things will never be quite the same.

My son also knows that this is the way things go. Change happens, usually in ways we can't control. You get used to it as best you can and try to look forward to what comes next. Losing a champion, though, is tough to take.

Personal Midwest
May 21, 2008

Last week, to celebrate our twenty-fifth wedding anniversary, my wife and I took a road trip to certain parts of our personal Midwest. Along the way, we looked forward to spending time with beloved friends and family members, as well as with certain favorite places.

Of course, a trip like this would also put us face-to-face with what's happened to gasoline prices in the past few months, not to mention what's come to be known as "America's crumbling infrastructure."

Needless to say, this ain't Jack Kerouac's America anymore. With the price for a gallon of fuel tickling $4, driving isn't cheap. Nevertheless, it looks more and more as if the high price of gas is a stand-in for this country's lack of an energy policy. What's more, it's actually starting to work.

Think about it: as driving becomes more expensive, people are becoming more thoughtful about when and where they drive. Not only that, they're apparently thinking differently about what they drive. Sales of SUVs have fallen dramatically. As we drove into St. Paul, Minnesota, we saw an aging recreational vehicle unceremoniously stopped by the side of a busy through street. It was easy to imagine the driver running out of gas and abandoning the guzzler, unable to face what it would cost to fill 'er up another time.

And in Madison, Wisconsin, I was almost run over by any

number of commuting bicyclists, a sign that even in a town where they put up with more than one hundred inches of snow last winter, people are opting for alternative forms of transport whenever they can.

Finally, wherever we went, from Milwaukee to Red Wing, folks were talking about the importance of the local food supply. With the cost of shipping produce from faraway places like California and Florida going through the roof, there's a greater incentive than ever to buy local. If this keeps up, we might actually put the "culture" back into agriculture again.

As for the roads ... I can't say they were better in Kerouac's day, but they couldn't have been much worse. It didn't matter where we drove—interstates, state highways, back roads, or city streets—axle busters were everywhere. Last winter, I know, was hard, especially from Chicago up through Minnesota. But it seems even harder to account for how it is so many roads in so many places have fallen into a gross state of disrepair.

If you go to the new Guthrie Theatre complex in Minneapolis, you can walk out onto an elevated deck that looks down the Mississippi River. From this vantage point, you can see the place where the 35W bridge collapsed last year. We heard people in the crowd around us pointing it out to their companions, murmuring things like, "There it is," and, "Look at that," and then falling quiet.

You see this and then, after the show, you get in your car and crack your teeth hitting a pothole in the middle of I-94. Let's say it makes you think.

For all the wear and tear, though, there's still something almost irresistible about getting behind the wheel and, as Mark Twain wrote, "lighting out." From Indianapolis to Minneapolis, the country was open, the skies were blue, and the water was fresh. Late one afternoon, we stood on the shore of our region's great inland sea, Lake Michigan, with a friend who told of seeing a white, freshwater pelican for the first time.

The next day we drove up Dylan's Highway 61, along the bluffs overlooking the Mississippi, a river so wide in places it made us wonder. It seemed like we were following spring. The redbud trees were almost done in Indianapolis, but they were blooming in Wisconsin. In St. Paul, it was just two weeks since Lake Como was covered with ice.

We were reminded that this great stretch of the Midwest is really a nation of its own. Everywhere we went there were backyards, clotheslines, and grills. Dandelions and, best of all, trees towering over the rooflines of houses in the neighborhoods where they grew.

A friend and I walked beside Lake Harriet in Minneapolis. He said the winter there had been "old fashioned," meaning brutal. But now it was gorgeous. People were everywhere—running, walking, biking—and no matter what they looked like or how old they were, you could tell they felt sexy. It was the middle of the week, but it seemed like Saturday.

Admiring the Amish:
Peanut Butter and Skepticism
April 25, 2012

If you travel to the northeast corner of Indiana, LaGrange County, to be exact, it won't be long before you find yourself in Amish country. In this part of the state, buggies are as common as automobiles. The public library in Topeka actually has two distinct parking lots, one for cars and the other for horse-drawn vehicles. On the Saturday afternoon I happened to be there, horse's hooves clip-clopping on the streets and the occasional whinny provided the ambient sound.

I must confess that the Amish are a mystery to me. I don't know what to make, for example, of their passion for peanut butter. Peanut butter, often cut with marshmallow paste or some other sweetener, is a cornerstone of Amish cuisine. They serve it at all manner of gatherings and get-togethers. Mention peanut butter and an Amish person's eyes light up. It's almost unnerving.

I have nothing against peanut butter. I've eaten it all my life. There is a jar of the stuff in my pantry now. It's the foot soldier of foods, as far as I'm concerned. Handy, but hardly a highlight.

That said, there is one aspect of Amish life for which I have an unqualified and increasing admiration. As far as I can tell, the Amish may be the only social group in America that isn't gobsmacked by technology.

Everyone, of course, is familiar with the stereotypical image of the Amish farmer plowing his field with a team of horses, or the families in those aforementioned buggies. But those are just the most outward signs of what seems to be a deeper skepticism about something the rest of us take for granted.

It's that skepticism that interests me.

We Americans, along with just about everyone else, have a long-running infatuation with gadgets. This took off with the Industrial Revolution. Machines changed the ways we lived and worked. They spurred the growth of cities, illuminated the night, and made overheated places cool. Machines extended human senses and reach. They effectively shrunk the planet, while investing individuals with a practically limitless sense of self.

So far, so good, right? That's certainly been the dominant culture's attitude toward the rise and development of new technologies. In part, that's because our inventions continue to drive the growth of our economy. We make stuff (or, at least, somebody does—in China, say, or Bangladesh) and then we buy it. Early adopters, those who are first in line for the newest phone or pad or operating system, are looked to as predictors of what will eventually be in store for the rest of us.

It's been this way for generations. We call it progress. Never mind that progress often means that things we used to think were important get atomized in the process. Many cities and towns, for instance, used to have bustling shopping districts where people gathered. But shopping malls and, more recently, online retailing, have sucked the air out of many downtowns and town squares, turning them into occasional destinations where, after business hours, the only things left to do are limited to dining in restaurants or attending a one-off sports or cultural event. Simply hanging out in these places is difficult, turning many of them into virtual ghost towns on weekends. But then, we have a term for this, too: "creative destruction."

When it comes to new technologies, our inclination has been to embrace them and ask questions later. Will ear buds make you deaf? Do cell phones cause brain cancer? Will sitting in front of a screen all day wreck your eyes? Since we haven't lived with any of these things through an entire human life cycle, nobody really knows. But such questions have been made irrelevant by our full-body embrace of these tools. Our homes and workplaces are now unthinkable without them.

All of this is not to say we should chuck our smartphones and laptops. We have enough trouble with e-waste as it is. Times, tools, and the behaviors they encourage are bound to change. I'd even go so far as to say our proclivity to lose our hearts to the latest algorithm may be one of our most endearing characteristics.

But, on a planet with limited resources and a growing population, it is also worth considering the extent to which this proclivity makes us prone to unintended consequences.

Our problem is that, when it comes to technologies, we don't know how to say no. There is nothing in our culture, no tradition or value system, to serve as a circuit breaker, saying, in effect, "don't go there," "you'll be sorry," or even, "maybe you should sleep on that."

This is why I admire the Amish. It's not that they are against technology. They actually use plenty of tools, and not just the nineteenth-century kind. Visit an Amish home and you're liable to be amazed by the conveniences they've managed to make room for. This doesn't make them hypocrites about technology. It makes them skeptical. I wish I could spread a little of that on a peanut butter sandwich.

'Tis the Season: Thanksgiving up North
December 2, 2009

When I was a little kid, Christmas won the holiday derby in a walk. Let me count the ways: there were snow, lights and colorful decorations, time off from school, and (drum roll) presents.

Almost as good as the presents themselves was the arrival every fall of the Montgomery Ward catalog. That thing was as thick as a big-city phone book, with every page in living color. The kids in my neighborhood pored over it, folding pages and circling items, making mental notes and dropping hints. Arriving in the mail as it did at just about the same time that darkness started falling at the unnatural hour of 4:30 in the afternoon, the Montgomery Ward catalog was, for a few weeks, at least, a hedge against what we later learned to call seasonal affective disorder.

I'm still nuts about Christmas. But, over the years, I think I've come to love Thanksgiving even more. I finally realized that last week.

We celebrated the annual feast up in Michigan City. As fate would have it, both my wife's folks and my own happen to live up there. The past couple of years haven't been easy for either set of parents. Health issues have made it increasingly difficult for one or another of them to get around. To tell you the truth, it's a gift that both couples are still with us.

On the other side of the spectrum, our son lives in Chicago, where he's been lucky enough to find a job. He has to work a lot of nights, and there's not much left in his wallet after he pays his share of the rent. But in an economy where roughly one out of every five young men between the ages of twenty-five and thirty-four is unemployed and a third of young workers in that age group are living at home, we're proud he's holding his own.

Anyway, thanks to public transportation—the Chicago South

Shore railroad, the last interurban train in Indiana—our son and Amy, his partner, were able to finish work Wednesday and be in Michigan City before dark.

Meanwhile, my wife and I picked up a fresh turkey at Goose the Market, packed up the dog along with the fixings for a traditional Thanksgiving dinner, and headed north on Highway 421. We've made this trip more times than either of us can count. At this time of year, the fields have been cut down to scrub and the trees are bare. You realize more than ever how big a part the sky plays in a midwesterner's sense of place. Whether it's low and stormy or high blue, it's a show that never quite repeats itself and never, ever, rests.

We did the cooking at my inlaws'. Everybody that could, chipped in. I know it's fashionable at this point in a holiday story to crank out a bit of snark about a cross-dressing cousin, glue-sniffing uncle, or munitions-dealing brother-in-law. Some grotesquerie to help rationalize our unwillingness or inability to find comfort in anything that might be called traditional. Sorry, but that's not the way it was.

At least not this year.

The fact is, we did a pretty good job of taking care of each other. The turkey was moist, the stuffing was amazing, the mashed potatoes had a whiff of rosemary, and, as usual, there were way too many sweet potatoes. We dimmed the lights in the dining room, and the grandfathers trailed off to nap to the white noise of a football game. Light from the kitchen washed over the faces of the grandmothers, who pulled up chairs in the doorway to watch as their young ones cleaned up.

The next morning there were leftovers to pack, a train to catch. The sun finally came out. My wife heard that the sandhill cranes were making their annual migration from Canada and the upper Great Lakes states. Each year at this time, from late September into December, thousands of these birds stop in the Jasper-Pulaski Fish and Wildlife Area before going on to parts of Florida. Since we were passing the refuge on our way home, she suggested we stop and have a look.

The sun was setting when we got there. We heard the cranes before we saw them: a great, raucous, choogling sound. The birds themselves are formidable. They stand over four feet high, and their wingspans can be as much as six feet across. There were thousands of them gathered on a green, marshy pitch, with hundreds more arriving in flocks from all directions.

The birds gather twice a day, at dawn and again at sunset, to call back and forth and to dance with one another. They flap their wings and jump up and down. This may be a form of courtship, but apparently there's also a chance they do it simply because it feels good, it's a bonding experience, and, yes, it gives them joy.

And they do it at Thanksgiving.

God Bless You, Mr. Vonnegut: And Farewell
April 18, 2007

It was snowing the morning that we heard Kurt Vonnegut died. Bits of snow blew through the open buds of our redbud tree like lost commuters wondering, "What are we doing here?"

In spite of the cold, peony shoots stood up in the garden, and the lawn, green as Ireland, was flecked with violets.

This was the sort of news I passed along to Mr. V when he called. Talking about the weather and what was blooming seemed a way of conveying the state of things in his hometown to him.

He had grown fond of this place.

One evening not that long ago, my son and I met Mr. V for dinner at a downtown hotel. As he came down the stairs, before so much as saying hello, with eyes wide, he asked, "Why did we ever leave Indianapolis?"

"So you could be an artist?" I asked in return.

Kurt Vonnegut's relationship to this city was complicated. It was a city his family helped build; a place where he claimed to have a happy childhood and a public-school education that he treasured. But his father, an architect, couldn't find sufficient work here, and his mother committed suicide. When Mr. V, arguably at the height of his powers, went to L. S. Ayres for a book signing in the late 1960s, it's said nobody showed up.

This, of course, changed. People waited for hours for the box office to open at Clowes Hall so that they might get tickets for the speech he was going to give this April 27. Many were disappointed when it quickly became clear that supply wouldn't come close to meeting the demand.

I met Kurt Vonnegut for the first time in Indianapolis, in 1991. He had agreed to be the keynote speaker at a book festival I organized called Wordstruck. Although I had read *Cat's Cradle* when I was in college, for some reason I hadn't picked up a Vonnegut book since. Maybe that was because he was everywhere, a ubiquitous part of the cultural landscape. At any rate, I was just hoping the guy it was my job to drive around town would be easy to get along with.

I had nothing to worry about. Mr. V was staying with childhood friends near Williams Creek. When I delivered him there, I was asked to come inside for lunch. This was a gift. The afternoon was spent drinking coffee, smoking cigarettes, and catching up. At one point our hostess leaned close to me and whispered, "He was such a beautiful boy, with the longest eyelashes I'd ever seen."

Needless to say, I began reading the books—all of them, as their author took justifiable pride in saying, still in print. Oh, what I'd been missing! There was the humor, that dark sense of human comedy and hapless mischief. But there was also Vonnegut's slapstick way of collapsing fact and fiction, like that boy he wrote about, roughhousing with his favorite dog on the living room carpet, as a way of seeking something like the truth.

And there was the voice. The voice above all.

Mr. V told me he learned to write when he worked for the Chicago News Bureau after the war, covering accidents and crime. The reporters called in their stories on the phone; they spoke, and someone on the other end typed the words. No wonder reading a Vonnegut book is like having the man himself by your side. That voice is what enabled an otherwise avant-garde artist to be embraced by a massive public. It made Kurt Vonnegut the literary equivalent of the Beatles.

Many people, even admirers, persist in calling Kurt Vonnegut cynical. I've never understood this. A cynic believes the truth doesn't matter. If going to war suits him, he'll make up reasons for doing it and to hell with the consequences. A cynic believes the only real crime is getting caught.

Truth, or at least our efforts to try and figure out what that means, always mattered to Mr. V. What he'd seen of human behavior made him a pessimist about the future we're making for ourselves. But this was also a man who, upon hearing of the almost inconceivably simultaneous deaths of his sister and her husband, responded by adopting three of their children. "There's only one rule I know of, babies," he wrote, "God damn it, you've got to be kind."

Tonight the sunset breaks through heavy clouds. Birds are singing in the crisp, platinum-colored air. I can imagine the smile this scene might put on Kurt Vonnegut's face, him calling out, "Get a load of this!" It's all he ever wanted us to really see.

Crossroads of America

Indianapolis was built at the center of its state, which is, if you close one eye and use a little imagination, located at the center of the country. As such, it became a hub for railroads and, later, the interstate highway system. What follows is a peripatetic set of localized responses to the ebb and flow of national events and cultural figures. Everyone from Oprah to Queen Elizabeth, Bob Dylan to Don Draper shows up. Eddie Haskell does a walk-on.

When Politics Was an Art: The Year I Discovered the Original JFK
November 3, 2004

Many people, including me, have remarked that this election we've just lived through may be the most important of our lives. We'll find out if that turns out to be true. The very idea, though, of elections as life-changing events makes one stop and think about the meaning of all those other elections that have taken place during the course of a given lifetime. The ones that really did make a difference.

For me, one stands apart from all the rest—and I didn't even vote in it. That was the election of John F. Kennedy in 1960. I was nine years old.

Needless to say, my fourth-grade political consciousness wasn't very sophisticated. But then it wasn't that different from many of the adults who were walking around in those days. I was attracted to JFK because of the way he looked. Of course looks, in Kennedy's case, amounted to more than met the eye. The man had a presence that was, at once, reassuring, worldly, thoughtful, and fun. I, along with a lot of other Americans, learned the meaning of the word charisma when Jack Kennedy came along.

That's a far cry from what passes for presidential today. Nowadays, the presidential job description seems to demand that a candidate be somebody most Americans would like having a beer with—somebody, in other words, who at least pretends to be just like them. Jack Kennedy made you want to be just like him.

Sure, it's true that many Americans detested Jack Kennedy. But it said something positive about this country at that time that so many of us—of all ages—looked up to the smart, well-bred picture he projected. In retrospect, it's easy to put this down, to say we were seduced by what were little more than images. But the words that went with those images never talked down to us. Kennedy made you want to be better than you were. He made that seem possible.

So I ventured out into the world that year and began collecting all of the red, white, and blue campaign paraphernalia that I could find. The buttons and stickers and posters that proclaimed Kennedy to be the future.

This took place in the northwest suburbs of Chicago, the other Cook County, where, I soon discovered, hardly anyone spoke Democrat. To give you some idea of what I was up against, four years later, when Lyndon Johnson waxed the national floor with Barry Goldwater in one of the biggest landslides in American history, my congressional district voted overwhelmingly Republican.

I was undeterred. I read everything I could about Kennedy, including the book about his exploits as a PT Boat commander during World War II, which in turn prompted the hit single by Jimmy Dean, the chorus of which concluded:

The PT 109 was gone,
But Kennedy and his crew lived on.

Meanwhile, most of my friends and classmates were building up their own collections of Nixon gear. This led to a lot of good humored, if high pitched, back and forth in the classroom, which led our teacher, the infelicitously named Mrs. Pynch, to turn the election into a teaching moment.

Mrs. Pynch called on the most outspoken advocates of both sides to make a presentation before the class in support of our favorite candidates. If memory serves, Bill Treece and Michael Wells, both of whom believed that old General Douglas MacArthur, the man who would have taken us to war with Red China, was really the only American truly fit for leadership, spoke for Nixon. I carried Kennedy's spear alone.

I knew the odds were against me, but I clung to the idea that, somehow, I'd prevail. I was dreaming. In what was to be a foretaste of politics to come, Nixon carried my classroom 23–9.

But I could take it. I went home and wrote a fan letter in my best cursive to JFK, thanking him for making politics come alive for me and wishing him luck. Then came the election—the closest, at that time, in American history. Thanks to the other side of Cook County, Kennedy won.

Two weeks later, a letter came to my house on John F. Kennedy For President stationary. It was typed and dated November 18, 1960. It read,

Dear Dave:

I wish to thank you for your recent letter regarding the election and for the interest you expressed. I regret that during the last few days of the campaign some of the mail was unanswered.

Again my thanks for your support which helped to insure this great victory. With your continuing help we will face each challenge which faces our nation successfully.

With every good wish, I am Sincerely,
John F. Kennedy

I am looking at that letter as I write this, noticing how the typewriter didn't strike quite cleanly on the letters 's' and 'p' and that the signature has faded somewhat to an almost colorless scrawl.

If it was amazing for me to receive that letter then (and it was), it seems even more remarkable today. People like to talk about how organized political campaigns have become, how computers and high technology have turned national races into a kind of science project. But once upon a time, the winner of the closest race the country had ever seen found the time to sign a letter to an American nine-year-old. I guess you could say that was when politics was a kind of art.

David Hoppe

1968 according to Theodore H. White
April 22, 2009

During the winter and spring of 1968, I went door to door in my politically conservative neighborhood, trying to drum up support for Eugene McCarthy's antiwar run for the presidency. I was in high school at the time, and, while I don't think I was able to rustle up many votes, I remember people being unfailingly courteous. I ushered at a rally McCarthy threw with Paul Newman at the Auditorium Theatre in Chicago. And it was my job to organize a rock dance at a suburban community center to round up teenage volunteers. Nobody but the bands showed up. We called it a night when a woman in her nightgown strode across the empty dance floor demanding we "turn it down!"

These were a few of the memories that came to me recently as I read a discarded library copy of Theodore H. White's *The Making of the President 1968*. I don't get the impression that people read White (who died in 1986) much anymore. But, for awhile, he had an extraordinary run, with a series of widely read books chronicling the presidential campaigns in 1960, '64, '68, and '72.

White's prose can seem a bit fusty and overwrought by today's standards. His tendency to believe that a country's character can be judged by the sophistication and accomplishment of its leadership also betrays an old-fashioned elitism that many contemporary readers might find quaint, if not off-putting.

But White was also a keen observer of how our politics play against America's larger cultural backdrop. I found that reading his on-the-ground reporting about the people and events of what turned out to be one of this country's most tumultuous years revelatory.

Part of the fascination of reading White's account of 1968 lies in what he couldn't know at the time. He is willing, for example, to accept the Johnson administration's account of the Gulf of Tonkin incident that Johnson used as pretext for escalation of the Vietnam War. In 2005 declassification of government documents proved the suspicions of antiwar activists that intelligence reports were jiggered to suit Johnson's desire to make war the way he wanted.

And White's inability to know what would become of Richard Nixon's looming presidency deepens his book's already tragic undertow. White admits that he didn't like the Nixon who ran for president in 1960. But he also believes that Nixon changed during his time away from politics. "None has shown himself, on the way to power, so susceptible to strain," White wrote, "yet apparently learned better how to cope with strain within himself…no passage of this public wandering has been more impressive than the transformation of the impulsive, wrathful man of the 1950's, so eager for combat and lustful for vengeance, to the man in the White House, cautious and thoughtful, intent on conciliation."

We know what White couldn't: about the infamous enemies list, the reliance on "dirty tricks," and, ultimately, the Watergate conspiracy. To White's credit as a writer, we read his portrait of Nixon and feel not just that Nixon has fooled White, but that, on a profound level and for a time, he probably fooled himself as well.

But Nixon's tragedy is yet to come. What White shows is that the full impact of Nixon's failure was tee'd up in 1968, by the unraveling of public trust in its political leadership. Lying optimism about the quagmire that was the Vietnam War, coupled with race riots in the cities and student protests on campuses and at the Democratic convention in Chicago, not to mention the murders of Martin Luther King, Jr. and Robert Kennedy, cracked the foundation on which our political culture was based.

White is particularly prescient when he writes about George Wallace's insurgent candidacy. "His message," wrote White, "was absolutely simple, short and clear. He was telling the people that their government had sold them out. Alienation is one of the more fashionable words in current American politics. It is the negative of the old faith that America was a community, and that government served the community. Alienation is disillusion…with the derivative that government must be seized and compelled to work…or ignored and overthrown."

Fragmentary resentments that were drawn to Wallace in 1968 would later coalesce to elect Ronald Reagan in 1980 and take over the Republican Party. Today, they are the so-called Republican base—the pissed-off, paranoid fraction of the electorate that's fueled by talk radio and Internet feedback loops. People who know what they're against, but can't say what they're for.

You have to wonder what White—whose attitude about race seemed to alternate between perplexity and despair—would have made of Barack Obama's candidacy. Surely, he never would have predicted it, but he would also have been attracted by Obama's intelligence, self-assurance, and grasp of the historical moment. He would also, given the wars that entangle us in Iraq and Afghanistan, the economic crisis at home, doubtless have offered Obama the same caution he offered Nixon: "He must make his way, certain of being abused whether rightly or wrongly, before his achievements permit sober judgment to be passed."

Songs of Experience:
Bob Dylan at the Egyptian Room
December 25, 2003

Tuesday, November 5, 2002, was an election day in the United States of America. All over this country, people were given the opportunity to exercise their franchise, to cast ballots for senators and governors and even county assessors. You'd think a day like this would represent a kind of snapshot of the national character at this particular time. The stakes couldn't have been higher. We were fighting a War on Terror, getting ready for another war with Iraq. While

TV commercials made it seem like there must be enough money for everyone to buy fast cars and perfect clothes, the facts were different. Fewer people could afford adequate healthcare. More people had to work two or even three jobs to get by.

But most of the people who could vote on this most American day of the year chose not to. And though the election said a lot about the influence that campaign contributors can buy, it told us very little about what it really means to live in this country at this time. For that information you best turn to a poet.

As it happened, Bob Dylan played the Egyptian Room on election night. What occult calculus was employed to position our country's living Shakespeare on an upstairs stage in the heart of the heart of the country at this of all times we might know but never fully understand. When, just a few weeks before, word came that Dylan would make Indianapolis a kind of rare club date, the news was greeted with incredulous joy. Why us? Why here? How typically Hoosier.

The date grew even more momentous with the passage of time. In Minnesota, not far from Dylan's Iron Range roots, Paul Wellstone, the kind of folk hero Dylan might sing about one day, was killed in a plane crash. With war looming and political discourse in the country all but shut down, this night in the Egyptian Room acquired a certain resonance.

Not that Dylan has made any real attempt to cultivate public perception of his significance. In fact, you could say that his last twenty years have been as much about deconstructing his 1960s "Voice of a Generation" persona as anything else. Embarked upon what's been called an "Endless Tour," the man seems intent on being known simply as a working musician and songwriter.

But, as we found out on November 5, it's through this latest incarnation that Dylan seems to have found his richest and, given the times, most disturbing voice.

To understand what Dylan's up to, arrive early. Like at most concerts, taped music plays through the hall before the artist takes the stage. In Dylan's case, though, the music playing is Aaron Copland. It's orchestral interpretations of American roots music, a modernist assertion of American folk culture's high art significance and, for Dylan, about as bold a statement of intention as you could ask for. In a gesture that, like so much of his work, is at once disconcertingly ironic and reverent, the last piece of music played before Dylan's band takes the stage is *Fanfare for the Common Man*.

As if this weren't enough, Dylan adds a final, icon-mocking touch: a spoken introduction that summarizes each phase of his forty-plus year career in purple *National Enquirer* prose—from prophet to substance abuser, to Christian convert to comeback trail. The inadequacy of these tags is hilariously clear. All of them are shortcuts, feeble attempts to brand the work without having to try and really understand it.

Maybe that's the point of the "Endless Tour." Dylan will perform for us until we finally get what he's been trying to do all these years. Not only that: he will keep performing because he, too, is finally getting what it's all about.

On stage, Dylan is lit from below. Dressed like a riverboat gambler by way of Salvador Dali, sporting a gigolo's mustache, Dylan looks like a character in a David Lynch fantasy. Except that Dylan was working on this character long before Lynch shot his first film. Now that he's sixty-one, it becomes increasingly clear that Dylan's project has probably always been about a search for the quintessential American character. It started when, barely more than a teenager, he sat by the dying Woody Guthrie's bedside. Then he went forth, making up an autobiography, including apocryphal stories of riding rails and a hobo life that belonged to Guthrie's generation.

Any great actor might have done the same. Somehow, though, Dylan's writing was confused with Beat-style personal confession. Throughout the '60s fans searched the songs like they were maps leading to genius. Little wonder this made Dylan uncertain and, at times, even resentful of his audience. In performance he all but mutilated his own material in an effort to find the voice that might finally crack his cult of personality. At the Grammys in 1991, in the wake of the Gulf War, he played "Masters of War," possibly as searing an antiwar song as has ever been written. But he played it jacked-up and slurred, as if to say: See? You've learned nothing. This means nothing. It seemed an act of despair.

Sir Laurence Olivier, the great English actor, played Shakespeare's tragic King Lear for the first time when he was in his thirties. People raved about Olivier's sheer ability to inhabit the body of an old man. But when Olivier played Lear again, in his seventies, he captured the king's soul in a way that moved audiences to tears. Olivier said the passage of time and his own aging had enabled him to truly grow into the part. Something similar seems to have taken hold of Bob Dylan. He was an old soul but still a young man when he wrote "Mr. Tambourine Man." Hear him sing it now. You realize this is not a song of innocence but of experience—and that Dylan is at last old enough to understand the song in a way he could only intuit when he first performed it.

The passage of time and experience has enabled Dylan to emerge as one of our great blues singers. The voice, splendidly ravaged, is a storyteller's dream. It seems to come from a timeless place that's equal parts café, shack, hotel room, and dirt road. He has spent a lifetime listening to the words America has used to brag, seduce, mourn, remember, and lie to itself. We listen to him and we hear our history as if picked up by some alchemical car radio during an all-night drive.

Now that he is no longer the leader, "the voice," Dylan is free to play a more significant and probably more enduring role. On another disappointing election night we saw it—and him—there before us. The wiry man in the dark suit sneered, but there was a sob in his throat. Whether he had been betrayed or had betrayed himself, there was, he seemed to say, enough blame in this country to go around.

David Hoppe

Hello, Vegas: America's Town
March 26. 2008

On the weekend that Bear Stearns, one of the largest investment banks in the world, was circling the drain, I was in, of all places, Las Vegas. It was my first visit to this city founded by gangsters, built on gambling, and dedicated to the proposition that reality can wait another day. I was eager to look around.

I mean, what better place to be as America stood on the precipice and stared into the abyss—or so I heard it said on CNN.

Back in the days of three-martini lunches and tailfins, Las Vegas was a devilish desert town, surrounded by an austere ring of mountains where ancient Indians left their handprints on the sheer faces of unforgiving rocks. As late as 1970, only 270,000 people lived there. They kept the food and lodging cheap and practically threw in the entertainment. The money was made on gambling, which was Vegas' main attraction.

Today, gambling is still a big deal in Las Vegas, but the city's business model has expanded considerably. Now gambling is just one dimension of a much larger package that sells itself as a full-service resort and convention destination—the ultimate escape.

There's nothing cheap about Vegas these days, but that's not to say the place has turned itself into a model of refinement and class. When you see the amount of money that has almost literally been poured into the creation of the temples of make-believe that line the Vegas strip—from a fake approximation of the Manhattan skyline to a pint-sized version of the Eiffel Tower—one thing becomes clear: Americans have a deep, if very guilty, love for hallucination.

Vegas, of course, is the place where we're supposed to set that guilt aside. And so you're encouraged to step into a gondola propelled by a guy in a striped shirt, which glides into a tunnel, that leads to a shopping mall, except this mall has a ceiling that looks like it was painted by Raphael, or Michelangelo, or one of those other Teenage Mutant Ninja Turtles. And then, if you go a little farther, you'll find yourself in the middle of an outdoor piazza, where people are dining in a sunlight that doesn't burn. Never mind that you're not actually outdoors. Or that it's not daytime.

Just never mind.

We stayed in a motel near the convention center on a street named Paradise Road. Paradise, in this case, had sidewalks so narrow it was difficult for people to walk two abreast without one risking being bumped into the path of some passing tour bus or truck. On our first morning we set out to find a breakfast place. A tourist map suggested that if we walked a mile or so we would find Vegas's old downtown, a place called Fremont Street. Surely, we thought, there would be a diner on the way.

It turned out the map's sense of scale, like everything else in town, was skewed. Fremont was much farther than indicated. Not only that, there was no place to eat en route. We did, however, see a slice of the Vegas that sucks the fumes from all the glitzier at-tractions—the dingy boxes on treeless streets where you can cash an out-of-state check, pawn your watch, have an "exotic" foot massage, or elope.

We found breakfast at a bar that opened early, sitting by a side-walk in the shadows of iconic old signs rescued from casinos and other businesses that didn't make the cut from old Vegas to new. These places were torn down, but their bright lights were installed on the street the way you would sculptures. It was as if, in the end, only the lights mattered.

When we got back to our room, I clicked on the television. CNN was calling the economy "Issue #1." There was a story about middle-class couples who couldn't keep up on their house payments and were living in trailers. Then they cut to Wall Street, where a close-up of a big board showed market values falling.

And there was mention of Bear Stearns.

From 2005 to 2007, *Fortune* magazine named Bear Stearns

America's "Most Admired" securities firm in its annual "America's Most Admired Companies" survey, a ranking that honors employee talent, management quality, and business innovation. The investment services company was founded in 1923 and known, among other things, for its colorful former chairman, "Ace" Greenberg, who sent his employees memos urging them to reuse paper clips and rubber bands—he suggested tying those back together if they were broken.

The news this day was that Bear Stearns, which in February traded at $93 a share, was to be sold to JP Morgan for $2 a share.

Now you see it. Now you don't.

Suddenly all America seemed like Las Vegas. And, this time, there was no pretending.

Economics according to Eddie Haskell: We're on Our Own

July 23, 2008

Remember a TV show called *Leave It to Beaver*? It ran from 1957 until 1963, and it's still on in reruns. The series was about growing up in the suburbs during the height of the Baby Boom. Every week Wally Cleaver and his little brother Theodore, better known as "the Beaver," got into some mortifying scrape. Once, on a dare, Beaver's head was stuck between the bars of a wrought-iron fence. Another time he found himself on top of a billboard in what was supposed to look like a steaming bowl of soup.

A recurring theme on *Leave It to Beaver* had to do with peer pressure. Beaver and Wally were constantly being tempted by their friends, the smarmy Eddie Haskell and his dim-witted sidekick, Lumpy Rutherford, to do things that put them in jeopardy. Luckily, our heroes' parents, Ward and June, were usually close at hand and could be counted on to get the boys out of whatever jam they'd gotten themselves into, albeit with a thoughtful scolding.

Ward and June, of course, were members of what has come to be known as "The Greatest Generation." Although we were never told what Ward did during the war, we could safely assume that he, like the rest of the dads in that neatly kept neighborhood, probably had a dress uniform in mothballs up in the attic. And though we never knew exactly what Ward Cleaver did to pay for the middle-class affluence his family enjoyed, we implicitly believed that every bit of it was earned thanks to the sacrifices in his generation's backstory.

If Ward and June were still alive today, they'd be shocked to see what their boys have done to the US economy. From the look of it, you'd think those kids never learned a thing.

Yes, it's as if Eddie Haskell has been in charge. Eddie was always looking for angles, shortcuts, the easy way out. As far as he was concerned, people were chumps. There was no rule of conduct that couldn't be bent or broken if it meant that Eddie gained an edge.

Eddie wouldn't have given a second thought to lending money to someone at terms they really couldn't afford—and then selling that loan to a bank too lazy to determine whether the loan was sound or not.

And Eddie would have bragged about how much it cost to fill his Hummer—he was always into conspicuous consumption.

Eddie would have been nudging Wally and Beaver in the ribs if they expressed doubts about the need to regulate financial institutions. "That's for saps," he would have said.

Eddie would have believed that markets take care of themselves.

Except that, as we are now finding out, that can mean a lot of people end up losing their homes, their savings, and their ability to pay for health care. A new report from the Center for Economic and Policy Research, "The Impact of the Housing Crash on Family Wealth," shows that the bursting housing bubble has had a devastating effect on the net worth of most American households. The combination of the fall of housing prices combined with low savings rates has left most Americans in the lurch, completely dependent on

Social Security and Medicare for their later years.

This wouldn't bother Eddie Haskell. No matter how many reckless deals he made, no matter how far in debt he slid, Eddie knew one thing: as long as he was spending other people's money, he'd be fine.

He knew this because he grew up in a world made by people like Ward and June Cleaver. If Eddie made a mess, the Cleavers, or someone like them, always bailed him out. Eddie knew the Cleavers would never let him fail.

But, as happened on most episodes of *Leave It to Beaver*, Eddie has forgotten something crucial: Ward and June and their entire generation aren't in charge any more. The Greatest Generation is trying desperately to hang on to what's left of its retirement.

It's the likes of Wally and the Beaver who have to put up with Eddie now. Wally's frowning and Beaver's scratching his head. When they look at Eddie, they both feel kind of used.

And you know what that means: uh-oh…

Taxes and Aliens:
Is It What We Pay or Who We Are?
May 5, 2010

Stephen Hawking, the astrophysicist and author of *A Short History of Time*, says we humans probably aren't the only life forms in the universe. According to an Associated Press report, Hawking recently told an interviewer that he believes intelligent aliens almost certainly exist. But, says Hawking, communicating with them could be "too risky."

Hawking likened a possible contact with aliens to Christopher Columbus's arrival in the New World, "which didn't turn out very well for the Native Americans." Hawking's guess is that most extraterrestrial life forms are microbial. But, he warns, more advanced forms might be "nomads, looking to conquer and colonize."

If this should ever come to pass, we might benefit by asking these new arrivals how the exploration that brought them here was funded. Were taxes involved? And, if so, were the other aliens back on Planet Zontar happy about it?

Taxes are a major bone of contention among we Earthlings, especially those living in these parts. You could argue that, without taxes, or, at any rate, the representation that supposedly accompanies them, there might not have been an American Revolution. "Taxation and representation are inseparably united," said Charles Pratt, Earl of Camden, in a speech to the British House of Lords in 1765. "God hath joined them; no British Parliament can put them asunder. To endeavor to do so is to stab our very vitals."

Had Pratt's colleagues been paying attention and allowed colonists to sit alongside them and vote in Parliament, we might now be worrying about the relative value of the pound versus the euro. Everyone would have health care, and our steering wheels would be on the right.

As we know, King George and Co. ignored Pratt's warning. America had its revolution. But our issues with taxation were only beginning. Flash forward to 2010, and a rolling boil with present-day tax protesters riffing on their eighteenth-century ancestors, calling themselves the Tea Party.

My *American Heritage Dictionary* defines "tax" this way: "A contribution for the support of a government required of persons, groups, or businesses within the domain of that government." Right away we have a problem. Those words "contribution" and "required" have a certain dissonance. A contribution implies a willing participation. But a requirement puts a coercive edge on it. Contribute or else.

Pratt's brilliant insight was to get that representation was a kind of bridge that made a tax seem more like a contribution than a requirement.

We have all kinds of taxes. There are property taxes we pay for the privilege of owning a house or business in a given governmental jurisdiction. There are sales taxes we pay on top of the price of things we buy, from gasoline to underwear. Sin taxes are charged for stuff we enjoy but might do us harm, like cigarettes and booze. And the income tax is a cut taken from our pay.

Taxes mean less money in our pockets.

But taxes also mean that someone picks up the phone when you call 911. Taxes pave the roads, build the schools, support a military, make sure our water is safe to drink, and see to it that people who are too old or infirm to work aren't entirely destitute. Taxes pay for the cleanup after natural disasters.

The need for some things, like roads and soldiers, seems obvious to people, and they contribute to these without much thought. But other items aren't as clear. Social Security and Medicare, food stamps and environmental protection, even schools: all of these have drawn fire from citizens who objected to being required to help pay for them.

Fair enough. These sorts of differences over what to pay for and why can and should serve as the bedrock on which a serious politics is based. Is, for example, health care a right or a privilege? That's a question worth debating and, ultimately, bringing to a vote. Indeed, determining the differences between rights and privileges is crucial to figuring out just what our social contract with one another is about.

But politicians, from both parties, have ducked this kind of debate. Instead, we hear about making health care "affordable," whatever that means, and about the need to reform the insurance industry.

We the people have enabled this lack of nerve. We've done this by rewarding politicians who stress taxes as requirements rather than contributions, who play to our living rooms instead of the public square. Rather than trying to decide what kind of society we want, we argue reductively at the margins over heroes and villains, who's up or down in the latest poll. In the end, nobody wins.

You have to wonder what those nomadic aliens Stephen Hawking conjures would make of us. Difficult as it is to picture them, it is even harder to imagine the discipline it would take for them to travel such a vast distance. They'd probably find us ripe for the picking.

The Ten Worst College Majors: And What's Even Worse

October 24, 2012

I was recently invited to serve on a committee. I am, as a rule, allergic to committees. While I realize their utility, I tend to agree with Groucho Marx, who once cracked that he didn't care to belong to any club that would have him as a member.

But this particular invitation came from my old alma mater, the college I attended back in those halcyon days when music was played on a stereo, term papers were pecked on typewriters—and practically everybody smoked.

The members of my class are having a reunion, and they've asked me to help plan it. I am still close to a number of my class-mates. We did a lot of growing together while we were in school, and, to the extent that some of us have stayed in touch over the years, this sharing of experience has continued through various and sundry break-ups, the growth of children, the loss of parents, and our own, inevitable aging.

So I'm looking forward to meeting up and hanging out with these friends of mine. I've begun to wonder, though, to what extent this sojourn is going to feel like a visit to some reservation for endangered species, where the lot of us will seem like so many marooned sea turtles.

We went to a liberal arts college. Most of us graduated with degrees in things like English, anthropology, sociology, and history. It was great. We learned a lot, like how to read and see and listen, and then how to think and talk about what it all meant. Many of us liked doing these things so much we kept at it, going to graduate schools and getting advanced degrees.

Most of us did all right. Not that we haven't screwed up here and there. But we're working, often in jobs that provide us with a decent amount of satisfaction and community impact.

The trouble is we keep hearing that the kind of education that enabled us to have the lives we do is on the way out. A recent study in the journal *Liberal Education* finds that many liberal arts colleges are either changing their missions or disappearing altogether. "Although many one-time liberal arts colleges cling to that historical identity in their mission statements and promotional literature, our findings confirm a continuing drift away from the traditional arts and sciences-based model of a liberal arts education," wrote the study's three authors, one of whom, incidentally, works for the accounting firm Ernst & Young.

In an article in the journal *Inside Higher Education*, Victor E. Ferrall, Jr., president emeritus of Beloit College, commented that, "the number of Americans who see the great value a liberal arts education provides is dwindling...In today's market, how is anyone going to get a job as an anthropologist or historian, let alone as a philosopher or expert in 19th-century English literature?"

As if on cue, *Forbes* magazine recently published a listing of the "10 Worst College Majors." The listing, calculated by the Center on Education and the Workforce (CEW) at Georgetown University, provides discouraging news about what liberal arts majors can expect employment and moneywise. Anthropologists between the ages of twenty-two and twenty-six are suffering a 10.5 percent unemployment rate and, if they do land jobs, a median salary of $28,000. "Non-technical majors—the arts (11.1%), humanities and liberal arts (9.4%), social sciences (8.9%) and law and public policy (8.1%)— generally have higher unemployment rates," states the *Forbes* report. "Conversely, health care, business, and the STEM fields (science, technology, engineering, math) have been more stable and higher paying for recent college graduates." Unemployment for nursing grads, according to *Forbes*, is just four percent; their median starting salary: $48,000.

"What society rewards in economic terms has moved away from the softer majors," says Anthony P. Carnevale, the director of Georgetown's CEW. "It's become about how much math you do."

I can easily imagine how a statement like this would have affected me when, as a high school sophomore, I was struggling to keep from flunking algebra. I would have sprinted down to shop class and splattered my math-intolerant brains all over the grease pit there with a tire iron. I'm sorry, but some—make that a lot—of us are not, nor will we ever be, equipped to build our lives around the ability to compute.

Besides, don't we have machines for that?

We Baby Boomers have been blamed for plenty of what's gone wrong with society over the past forty years or so, from recreational sex to SUVs. But what I want to ask my compadres planning our college reunion is this: Why are we failing to preserve a way of education that enabled us to have the kinds of lives we enjoy today?

The liberal arts introduced us to timeless questions about who we humans are and how we live together. Then they provided the tools necessary to explore these things in ways that, if they haven't necessarily made us rich, have enriched us. When we found these traditions, they were vibrant and alive; we seem to have reduced them to columns in a cost-benefit analysis. You'd think we would have learned to pass along more than that.

What Boomers Did to College Ed.: We Came We Saw We Wrecked It
December 19, 2007

From civilized air travel to the nuclear family, the Baby Boom generation has laid waste to a lot of things that used to make this country great. I'm a member of that generation, so I should know.

Even I, however, am astounded by the mess we Boomers have

made of the one thing that set us apart from previous generations, giving us advantages they could only dream about: the college education.

Before the Baby Boom, it was considered a rare privilege to have a college degree. I remember my sixth-grade teacher, Mrs. Ryder, asking us to raise our hands if we expected to go to college. When almost everyone in class obliged, Mrs. Ryder told us this meant that many of us would be the first ones in our families to cross this threshold. This, she said, was part of the American story in which each generation paved the way to make life better for the generation that came after.

In the 1960s higher education was one of America's biggest growth industries. Since there were more kids than ever before, this meant more teenagers enrolled in colleges and universities. There were actually television commercials aimed at encouraging people to go to college. One showed a guy jumping into a swimming pool with a pair of lead boots on his feet. The not-so-subtle message was that, without a college degree, he was never going to get a good job.

So off to college we Boomers went. And guess what? We liked it there. In fact, we liked it so much, many of us stayed—first to pile on a graduate degree or two, and then to stake a claim as teachers and administrators. Campus life, it turned out, offered charms not easily come by in what we called "the Real World."

Being Baby Boomers and priding ourselves on our advanced social consciousness and talent for innovation, we proclaimed that our love for things academic was a good thing—for the colleges and universities, of course. We would reinvent, update, and expand these crabby old institutions. And, in so doing, we would do away with that old bugbear about those who can doing and those who can't teaching. Indeed, we set things up so that many so-called professors never even had to enter a classroom! There were graduate students for that.

Yes, we took that growth industry and corporatized it.

It comes as no surprise, then, to wake up to recent headlines about the billion-dollar endowments our colleges and universities are amassing while, at the same time, they charge more than ever for tuition. According to the College Board, college prices have risen 35 percent in just the past five years. Since 1992 increasing college costs have outgrown family incomes for all but the 20 percent of American families with the highest incomes. Although student financial assistance from all sources has increased by 140 percent since 1991, it hasn't come close to keeping pace.

A 2006 report called "Mortgaging Our Future" by the Advisory Committee on Student Financial Assistance found that, in the 1990s, up to 1.5 million academically qualified low- and moderate-income students with college aspirations did not earn bachelor's degrees within eight years of high school graduation because of financial barriers. As many as 2.5 million students are expected to be in the same boat during this decade.

But that's not all. Among those students who are able to attend college, only about two-thirds complete a bachelor's degree in six years. According to "Measuring Up," a 2006 study by the National Center for Public Policy and Higher Education, the United States ranks sixteenth in completion rates among twenty-six nations internationally. The "Measuring Up" study finds that American higher education is underperforming in preparing the next generations to replace retiring Boomers; in creating an internationally competitive workforce; and in maintaining and enhancing opportunity and upward mobility for young Americans.

What's especially galling about this is that in all the talk about the high cost and under-performance of American higher education, there is little or no discussion about how our colleges and universities are actually run. The hierarchies, privileges, and fiefdoms that define our academic institutions are well known to anyone that's ever spent time around a campus. These cultural peccadilloes, along with the conventional wisdom that schools must model themselves along the lines of resort spas in order to compete for students, are treated like forces of nature rather than the self-congratulatory indulgences they really are.

Baby Boomers came of age on campuses. Then we took over. It's been a nice ride for some —nothing less than the chance to live in an alternative universe. But if Mrs. Ryder were alive today, I doubt she'd say we'd made life better for anyone but ourselves.

Right-Wing Snake Oil:
David Horowitz Sells It
April 20, 2005

A couple of weeks ago, David Horowitz took a pie in the face at Butler University. Horowitz is a right-wing con man, a guy who has found a lucrative career testing the boundaries of politically acceptable thought. Horowitz's job in the political scheme of things is to find out how gullible we are. Karl Rove, President Bush's so-called "brain," is an admirer of Horowitz's work.

Horowitz was at Butler pushing what he calls an Academic Bill of Rights. For the past couple of years, Horowitz has been working hard to do for the world of colleges and universities what he and his cronies have successfully managed in the world of media. That is, convince people that a hierarchical, tradition-bound institution is a leftist hotbed of anti-American radicalism.

Horowitz, who uses something called the Center for the Study of Popular Culture as a front, has been campaigning in person and via the Web to expose what he calls a "corruption of academic integrity." He cites "recent studies" by "independent researchers" that purport to show "that on any given university faculty in America, professors to the left of the political center outnumber professors to the right of the political center by a factor of 10–1 and more." Horowitz does not say where these studies come from, but after doing some digging, Dr. Graham Larkin of Stanford University has found that it appears Horowitz is connected to this so-called independent research.

Horowitz says that college students today are being oppressed by the liberal bias of their professors. On the one hand, he says that he wants to depoliticize the campus: "We do not go to our doctors' offices and expect to see partisan propaganda posted on the doors, or go to hospital operating rooms and expect to hear political lectures from our surgeons. The same should be true of our classrooms and professors, yet it is not."

But then, in the name of "diversity," Horowitz advocates ideologically polarized, right-left litmus tests that would affect virtually all areas of academic life, including grading, curriculum development, selection of invited speakers, allocation of funds, hiring, firing, and tenure review. What's more, Horowitz is encouraging legislators in a number of states, including Indiana, to link funding for state schools to the implementation of the Academic Bill of Rights.

Horowitz has used his Center for the Study of Popular Culture as a vehicle for the creation of a supposedly grassroots and conveniently Web-based student movement called Students for Academic Freedom. SAF, it turns out, is linked to the American Legislative Exchange Council, a right-wing group founded by Paul Weyrich and funded by corporations like Coors, Phillip Morris, and Exxon that works to develop and pass special-interest legislation.

Horowitz knows from experience that if you rant about something long enough, people will believe that what you say is true. For example, he continues to complain about the "liberal media" when many of his right-wing colleagues have already declared victory. Bill Kristol of the *Weekly Standard*, himself hit with a pie at DePauw not long ago, has said, "I admit it, the liberal media were never that powerful…" Or Rush Limbaugh: "There's been a massive change in the media in this country over the last 15 years. Now it's 2002 and the traditional liberal media monopoly doesn't exist anymore." In the 2000 elections, American newspapers endorsed Bush over Gore by a 2–1 margin and, according to a survey in *Editor and Publisher* magazine, a large majority of the nation's newspaper editors and publishers said they voted for Bush themselves. As Adam Meyerson of the

Heritage Foundation has noted, "Today, op-ed pages are dominated by conservatives…"

Ironically, at the same time that Horowitz is leading a charge to redefine the meaning of academic freedom from a right-wing perspective, ties between big corporations and universities are stronger than ever. Corporate funding for university research has seen a seven-fold growth since 1970. As that anarchist bomb-thrower Alan Greenspan has said of corporate-university partnerships, "The payoffs, in terms of the flow of expertise, new products and startup companies…have been impressive."

This research covers a wide variety of disciplines and has raised serious concerns about academic independence and conflicts of interest. A Tufts study of eight hundred scientific papers published in major biology and medical journals found that in one out of three cases the chief author of the paper had a financial interest in the company for which the research was being done. A study by the Center for Biomedical Ethics at Stanford found that 98 percent of university studies of new drug therapies funded by the pharmaceutical industry reported that those therapies were more effective than standard drugs. But just 79 percent of studies without industry financing found the new drugs to be more effective.

So at the same moment that David Horowitz would have us believe that our campuses are in the grip of leftist fiends, these same campuses are also becoming research and development centers for the world's biggest corporations. And, by the way, tuition everywhere is going up—making a college education less available to regular folks than ever.

Does that sound like creeping socialism to you? If your answer is yes, David Horowitz has a bridge to sell you.

Waiting for Superman? Education Can't Work without Culture
November 19, 2010

On the first day of my freshman year in high school, my English teacher, Miss Hurcik, asked us to write a short essay on that classic theme, "What I Did on My Summer Vacation." I was eager to show my new teacher what I could do. I wasn't that hot at math, but in junior high the teachers encouraged me to write. I figured this was my chance to shine.

I wrote about a trip my parents and I took to the Gettysburg battlefield in Pennsylvania. I described the place and its history. As I recall, I finished by trying to express how the experience made me feel.

I felt pretty good about that essay.

Sure enough, when Miss Hurcik returned the paper to me, it was marked A at the top. But there was a note at the end that made my blood run cold. It said I was getting the A because Miss Hurcik couldn't prove that I'd cheated on the assignment. Next time, though, I'd better not copy someone else's work.

It took me a year to get over being punished, in effect, for doing the best I could in school. If another teacher, Miss Trout, hadn't discovered me in my sophomore year and reassigned me to her fast-track world history class, I'm not sure what would have happened to me.

Miss Trout's world history class was a revelation: I found out that life was a lot easier in a fast-track class than in the slow and average classes. In the fast-track classes, kids raised their hands and listened to one another; teachers were on their side. Whereas, in one of my slow math classes, a kid actually threw his desk at the teacher. I sat in the back row and tried my best to make myself invisible.

Thanks to Miss Trout, I found high school's promised land.

One fast class led to another and, when I satisfied that math requirement at the end of sophomore year, I found myself actually looking forward to school, instead of dreading it.

All this came to mind after watching *Waiting for Superman*, the documentary film about the mess we've made of our educational system. *Waiting for Superman* makes a strong case for the impact teachers can have on students' lives. At one point, the educator Geoffrey Canada compares great teachers to great artists. It's a powerful analogy.

Great teachers, like great artists, are both gifted and highly disciplined. Their craft is based on a mastery of knowledge and technique, enabling them to come up with creative solutions to problems in a variety of situations, and to bring fresh insight to familiar materials.

But what Canada leaves out of his analogy is that great artists are, in fact, rare. More artists are good than great, and many, many more than that are merely satisfactory. It's important to remember this, particularly when we consider what should constitute teacher training. The master of fine arts programs that have sprung up in colleges and universities across the country have enabled more people than ever to write decent short stories and make passable paintings. True masterpieces are scarce as ever.

Waiting for Superman casts a rueful eye back to American schools in the 1950s and '60s. This, the movie as much as says, was the golden age of American public education. Compared to what we have today, it's hard to disagree.

But if the quality of education during the Baby Boom era was preferable, it wasn't because teacher colleges were turning out an army of master teachers. For every Miss Trout, there was a Miss Hurcik.

The difference was the curriculum. Baby Boomers, no matter where they went to school, all studied essentially the same subjects, consisting of similar content. When I entered college, in 1969, I found that my peers, whether they came from Grand Forks or Boston, Seattle or Baton Rouge, had all read pretty much the same books and had similar stories to tell.

Today, you'd be hard-pressed to find this kind of cultural consistency among schools in the same city.

To the extent that our schools worked, it was because there was a general—make that cultural—agreement about what constituted a sound education. Was this agreement reductive? Certainly. Did it allow for a variety of learning styles? Hardly. It was also far too hierarchical, authoritarian, and triumphal. That's why we started dismantling it in the '70s.

We're nowhere near reaching the kind of cultural consensus about what constitutes an education that made our system work following World War II. We've substituted choice for consensus, and that's proven to be a shallow, at times even brutal, alternative. That we put kids and parents through the lottery process shown in *Waiting for Superman* is nothing short of barbaric.

I was lucky. Though Miss Hurcik did her worst, Miss Trout was there to help bring out my best. Both teachers worked within a common system that made navigation possible. We don't have that now. Don't count on education getting better in this country until we do.

Educational Testing: Just another Job
January 5, 2011

I had a real Wizard of Oz moment the other day—make that a *Wicked* moment, if you prefer. You know the wizard's story: he's a fake who hides behind a curtain, dishing meaningless bromides to his subjects in the Emerald City so they'll think he's got some sort of special mojo.

The moment I'm talking about came courtesy of a writer named Dan DiMaggio, whose article, "The Loneliness of the Long-Distance Test Scorer," was published in December's *Monthly Review* magazine

For the past three years, DiMaggio has worked as a test scorer, reading and scoring the written-response portions of the kind of standardized tests given to millions of American third to twelfth graders. The work is seasonal, usually lasting around four months of any given year.

DiMaggio, who lives in the Twin Cities, says he has personally read tens of thousands of papers, for which he has been paid at a rate of 30 to 70 cents per paper. That means he has to score forty papers every sixty minutes in order to make $12 an hour.

DiMaggio's article was a revelation to me. Although I've never been a great fan of standardized testing and am particularly skeptical about the increasing faith politicians, business leaders, and bureaucrats seem to have in it, I also understand that these tests can, in fact, serve to provide us with one, very general, indicator about how kids are doing in school.

What never occurred to me was that rather than being an objective and impartial reflection of a student's educational attainment, these tests are yet another form of boiler-room toil, subject to the flaws and foibles of our growing population of overeducated, underpaid American schmoes.

I worked in a boiler room once. I was a telephone solicitor, trying to sell people *Time-Life* books about the Wild West. A bunch of us of sat behind heavily bruised steel desks in an office above Market Street in San Francisco. On those desks were a hunk of phone book for the area code each of us was supposed to call and an ashtray. The only other furnishing in the room was a Coke machine. The job involved calling over one hundred phone numbers every hour.

It turns out something similar happens with the tests our kids take at school. "In test-scoring centers, dozens of scorers sit in rows, staring at computer screens where students' papers appear...each scorer is expected to read hundreds of papers," writes DiMaggio. "So for all the months of preparation and the dozens of hours of class time spent writing practice essays, a student's writing probably will be processed and scored in about a minute."

Since scorers are paid per paper—and since there are only so many papers overall—scorers are in a race against their coworkers to do as many papers as they can. DiMaggio says this resulted in contradictory messages from the testing company, warnings, for example, that he was scoring too fast, with simultaneous messages that his group was way behind.

DiMaggio writes, "Unfortunately, after scoring tests for at least five states over the past three years, the only truly standardized elements I have found are a mystifying training process, supervisors who are often more confused than the scorers themselves, and a pervasive inability of these tests to foster creativity and competent writing." According to DiMaggio, testing companies' "ultimate goal is to present acceptable numbers to the state education departments as quickly as possible, beating [the departments'] deadlines…"

It's a numbers game. And the thing about numbers is that if they're too low or too high they won't be considered reliable. "Usually in a day or two, when the scores we are giving are inevitably too low (as we attempt to follow the standards laid out in training), we are told to start giving higher scores," writes DiMaggio. "For some mysterious reason, unbeknownst to test scorers, the scores we are giving are supposed to closely match those given in previous years."

Meanwhile, some kid, or some teacher, is going to be judged based on whether or not those test scores are up to par. DiMaggio writes that scorers can never know how students are affected by the scores they get. "Whether Marissa will be prevented from going to seventh grade with her friends because one of us, before our first cup of coffee kicked in, decided that her paper was 'a little more like a 3 than a 4…' Whether Marissa's school will be closed or her teachers fired (to be reborn as test scorers next spring?) remain mysteries to the test scorers."

We've substituted testing, the illusion that numbers never lie, for the hard work of deciding what an education should be. Rather than reform, our fixation on educational testing is a default setting, the cultural failure to agree on whether our kids should be taught or merely trained. That's why the next time I hear our schools described in terms of test scores, I'll think of the Wizard of Oz—the test scorer behind the curtain.

In the Land of the Working Stiff
June 27, 2007

It's summer, time for baseball, so the other night I went to a game at Victory Field. It was a gorgeous evening, the western sun casting a golden glow upon the bland faces of downtown office buildings and hotels. I had a beer and a hot dog and watched the ballplayers warming up. Then, along with everybody else, I stood for the singing of the "Star-Spangled Banner."

You know how it goes: "Dawn's early light…perilous fight…" Momentum builds and then we get to the climax, which is actually a question: "O, say does that star-spangled banner yet wave, o'er the land of the free, and the home of the brave?"

Stirring stuff.

A lot of people complain about the "Star-Spangled Banner." They say it's too hard to sing, but I've never had a problem with it. The only part of the song that gives me pause is that last line, the bit about "the land of the free."

That's because when I looked around the ballpark at all the people there, I knew I was seeing members of the most overworked population in the industrialized world. According to the United Nations' International Labor Organization, Americans work 250 hours, or five weeks, more than our counterparts in Great Britain, and 500 hours, or twelve and a half weeks, more than those infamous layabouts, the Germans. Every European has the right to at least twenty days of paid time off per year—some get as many as twenty-five or thirty days. The Swedes get thirty-two.

The average American vacation is now a long weekend. Our Bureau of Labor Statistics tells us that one in four of our workers gets no paid vacation at all, and—here's the real kicker—fifty-one million Americans, or a third of our workforce, won't take all the vacation days they have coming. Each worker will pass up an average of three days off.

I don't know about you, but this does not look like "the land of the free" to me.

I'm sure that if you were to ask a CEO about this—somebody, that is, who's making seventeen times more than most of the people working for him—that person would tell you people in America work as much as they do because, darn it, working long hours (and staying away from the family as much as possible) is the American Way.

But if you compare the quality of life in the USA with other industrial countries, you quickly see that when it comes to health, savings, and social equality, the US has fallen behind. This is a country where job security is scarce to nonexistent, where health care without job-connected insurance has been unaffordable, and where the so-called social safety net has been systematically dismantled. It's no wonder we take more antidepressants than anyone else and get divorced as often as we do. In America, that's what we call a party.

Of course, we keep these cracks from showing by consuming lots and lots of stuff. Today, each American, on average, consumes fifty-three times more "goods" than a citizen in China, where so much of the stuff we consume is made. This has been a trend in American life going back to the days after World War II, when the president of the National Sales Executives declared, "Capitalism is dead—consumerism is king," meaning that our economy would no longer be driven by what we built so much as by what we bought. We've been living on credit, something frowned on before 1941, ever since.

As any smoker knows, there's an addictive quality to living like this. You can call it freedom if you want, and many people do, even as they're picking through ashtrays looking for butts because they've run through their last pack. Even France, which used to have a thirty-five-hour work week, is not immune. They just elected a new president, Nicolas Sarkozy, whose motto is "work more, earn more." The problem is that longer hours often mean that wages stagnate or fail to keep up with inflation. That's what's happened here. Most Americans need two-income households just to stay even.

That's not all. It appears that overwork is bad for the environment. A study by the Center for Economic and Policy Research in Washington, DC, suggests that if Europe adopted America's working ways, it would consume 15 to 30 percent more energy by 2050. This would boost carbon emissions and cause additional global warming of 1 to 2 degrees Celsius. Any gains made through conservation, green technologies, and cleaner fuels would be rubbed out.

Never mind about that, though. Now that all of us are living so much longer—well beyond the ability of most of us to squirrel away enough for an extended retirement—there's even more work to look forward to. That's the land of the free, all right; the home of the working stiff.

Gay Marriage and the Next Big Thing…Gay Divorce
June 25, 2008

You could practically hear the sounds of celebration coming out of California last week as gay and lesbian people there reveled in the newfound right to be legally married. Not only were the newlyweds whooping it up, the people who make money from tourism and special events were popping a few corks of their own. Spending for same-sex weddings in California, which will include out-of-state couples as well as residents, is expected to add over $683 million to California's economy over the next three years.

All anyone with doubts about the validity of gay marriage had to do was think about the journey of Phyllis Lyon and Dorothy Martin. This octogenarian couple has been together for fifty years. In 2004, when San Francisco's mayor, Gavin Newsom, impetuously declared gay marriage legal within his city limits, they were first in line for a ceremony, only to see their status flipped by the courts. Now, with a new state supreme court ruling on their side, they were back at City Hall, determined to make honest women of one another.

Good for them. And good for California for understanding that all people are created equal, meaning we all deserve an equal chance to pursue happiness and, it must be said, to screw up. The latest thing may be gay marriage, but, as long we're alluding to self-evident truths, let's face this one: gay divorce is next.

Just ask those wedding planners who are already reserving exotic vacations with the profits they plan on making from the gay marriage bonanza. They'll tell you that everybody loves a party. And nothing says blowout like a dream wedding. A funny thing happens when some people decide to get married; they use the occasion less for a public declaration of the commitment they're making to one another than as a celebration of self. All that's missing at some of these fandangos are a team of cheerleaders and a homecoming parade.

Weddings like these aren't the beginning of something, so much as the high-water mark for a lot of relationships. It's all downhill after that. It's no wonder that someone in this country gets divorced every ten to thirteen seconds.

This is what makes the protestations of the Defense of Marriage people seem so ludicrous. When you look at what we heteros have done to the institution, if anything, you want to welcome gays aboard in the hopes that maybe they'll set a good example.

Trouble is, when it comes to basic things like marriage, our fundamental equality suggests that gays will be as prone to post-nuptial remorse as anyone else. According to the US census, the odds are that almost one out of every two younger American adult couples who marry for the first time will wind up being divorced.

And it doesn't help if they live together before tying the knot. It isn't just their sexual preference that makes that old San Francisco couple, Ms. Lyon and Ms. Martin, a minority. Their commitment and unabashed dependence on one another are what make their love story truly rare. If they stay together from here on out, they will be exceptions yet again, because most couples who live together before marrying wind up splitting.

Now that gay marriage is legal in California, gays will face the increased risks of mental and physical problems associated with marital distress. A variety of studies going back to the 1980s indicate that people's health is one of the first things to go when their marriage hits the skids.

Oh, and that windfall California plans on collecting thanks to the gay marriage boom could also be a mixed blessing. If gays are like the rest of us, their marital problems can be expected to result in the same decrease in work productivity that has been observed in broken-hearted heteros. So much for economic development.

You have to wonder that our gay brothers and sisters are still willing to make this leap of faith. Yes, there are certain legal advantages to be had, but, for many of us, these have never been enough to keep divorce at bay. In the end, the story here is really about freedom. Real freedom isn't just about success; it grants the right to fail—to everyone.

And so, my gay friends, welcome to matrimony!

Obesity Epidemic:
Don't Blame the Media
February 15, 2006

Well, whatever else you might say about the epidemic of obesity that's sweeping Indiana and the nation, it's hard to blame it on the media. Unless our society is honeycombed with saturated cells where people are secretly gorging themselves on *Roseanne* reruns and old Fatty Arbuckle comedies, it's hard to see what reinforcement TV, magazines, or movies are providing to the overweight. As anyone who partakes of our popular culture will tell you, it's a nonstop festival of thin.

But apparently that doesn't keep people from reaching for another slice of pizza while they watch VH1's 100 Greatest Celebrity Bodies.

Something weird is going on here, especially for bleeding hearts like me who want to believe that communication not only matters, but that the messages we fill our society with go a long way toward defining who we are and what we do. No advertising agency in the world could design a more comprehensive campaign than the one we have going every day on behalf of being slender. We are immersed in images of movie stars, supermodels, and athletes.

So what do we do?

We ask for seconds.

Those of us, for example, who believe that the gratuitous and graphic depictions of sex and violence used to attract eyeballs and sell beer and fast food have a corrosive effect on our communities have to think again. Instead of leaping to the conclusion that what we see can be reduced to the cause for a particular effect—that playing violent video games, let's say, triggers violent behavior—we may need to shift our focus.

The medium, McLuhan said, is the message. In other words,

delivery systems matter more in terms of how we understand who we are than the discreet messages they carry. The presence of a television, or two or three, in your house matters more than a public service campaign aimed at encouraging you to go out and take a walk around the block.

Electronic media change the way we think and feel about ourselves, our communities, and the messages we send to one another. You can see this in our politics. People (usually older people, that is) wonder what's happened to political activism and the kinds of demonstrations that tilted the balance of power in favor of civil rights a couple of generations ago. They wonder how it is that so many of us stand by while our government enacts policies regarding the environment, education, and health care so plainly not in our best interest. There's no lack of information about these things. Where's the outrage?

It's at home, in front of the tube or the computer screen. Kurt Vonnegut once quipped that people have come to confuse watching TV with citizenship. The same can be said for those of us who spend our time trolling the web for information with which we agree and calling it activism.

The trouble with the rampant exploitation of sex and violence in the media may not be that it causes people to behave in antisocial ways, but that it causes nothing at all. That, in fact, it is part of a desensitizing process that strips the power from art and threatens to make communication meaningless. Violence in the real world is a byproduct, the side effect of a much larger, and deeper, assault on identity.

Why, in spite of all the messages they get to the contrary, are so many kids becoming obese? Junk food and sputtering parenting skills certainly have something to do with it. And cutting gym class from the schools' curriculum certainly hasn't helped. But if we're to get to the root of this problem, we're going to have to take a hard look at the larger medium these kids are growing up in.

We've created an economic system that prizes growth above

everything else. "Grow or die" is the mantra of American capitalism. In order to grow and feed the ever-expanding appetites of shareholders and consumers, globalization has become the justification for outsourcing jobs and shrinking or reneging on salaries and benefits. Growth has demanded that we use more energy regardless of cost. That's ok. Growth, we say, equals progress.

But growth of this sort is really just a numbers game. Fixating on size overlooks the complex web of ways a business interacts with and enriches its community and environment. I know how squishy that sounds, but before you put this column on the bottom of your birdcage, consider this: greenhouse gas concentrations in our atmosphere are around 380 parts per million. In the last ice age, they were 220 ppm. Climatologists estimate that if we reach 400 ppm, dangerous climate change could become irreversible. The earth is looking like an overweight twenty-year-old with clogged arteries and poor circulation.

The planet's future depends on whether our business and government leaders have the will to adapt and develop new ways of understanding growth. The same thing can be said about our kids. I wish we could blame the media for these problems. Then, maybe, the media could fix them.

Making Love without Making Babies: America after the Pill
July 6, 2011

There's an old joke about the 1960s: people may not have invented sex in those days, but it often felt like they did.

The combined oral contraceptive pill, better known simply as "the pill," received FDA approval in 1960. Contraception in some way, shape, or form goes back to the Stone Age. But the pill changed the way people thought about and experienced sex. It put the focus on pleasure instead of procreation.

This was a Very Big Deal. It seems almost inconceivable now, but until the pill came along, the notion that pleasure wasn't just a byproduct of sexual intimacy, but could actually be an end in itself, was radical. Earlier in the twentieth century, writers like D. H. Lawrence and Henry Miller were considered revolutionary for espousing the liberating qualities of getting it on; their works were duly driven underground or into courtrooms, where they were put on trial for obscenity.

In fact, although the pill surfaced in 1960, it took more than a decade and a Supreme Court decision before it was available to single people throughout the country. In 1972, in *Eisenstadt v. Baird*, the Supreme Court found that unmarried people had the same right to contraception as married couples. William Baird was charged with a felony under Massachusetts' "Crimes Against Chastity" act for distributing contraceptive foam during a lecture he gave on population control at Boston University. The court ruled that the Massachusetts law denied citizens equal protection and violated their privacy. In effect, it also created the sense that consenting adults had what amounted to a right to engage in sexual activity that had nothing to do with making babies.

Eisenstadt v. Baird is worth remembering in light of the recent attacks on Planned Parenthood. Many observers have seemed bewildered by right-wing insistence on cutting off Planned Parenthood's funding over the issue of abortion, when abortion plays such a small role in the organization's larger mission of providing family planning and health services to women in need. Defenders of Planned Parenthood have argued that these attacks represent an assault on lower-income women, which is true.

But these are also attacks on the belief that it's OK to make love without making babies. *Eisenstadt v. Baird* reminds us that not that long ago, in many parts of the United States, there were laws preventing anyone but married couples from getting access to the pill. Many

Americans, including current majorities in the Indiana House and Senate, apparently still believe that sex should be understood strictly within the context of procreation and marriage.

It seems odd that we don't talk more about how some of the forces arrayed against an organization like Planned Parenthood are really against sex for its own sake. But then we Americans are notoriously tongue-tied when it comes to talking about our sexuality. If you doubt this, look at how we try to compensate for our lack of candor.

We've turned pornography into an all-access branch of the entertainment industry. Porn is the proving ground for imagery that finds its way into the ever-more permissive realm of mainstream movies, television, and advertising. It used to be that people argued that schools needed to teach sex education since parents were too bashful to do it themselves. Now, in addition to parental embarrassment, the schools are faced with trying to offset porn-fueled pop culture.

We would doubtless like to think that our tolerance for pornography indicates a larger liberation when it comes to sex, that our willingness to be amused, aroused, and (secretly) instructed by porn is proof of how comfortable we've become in matters of sexual intimacy. But it seems just as possible that the opposite is the case, that pornography is a marker for loneliness and that, when it comes to lovemaking, we're still pretty confused.

It wasn't long after the *Eisenstadt v. Baird* ruling that the so-called Sexual Revolution reached full flower in the United States. The realization that sex and babies could be a choice and not a consequence created a temporary euphoria. For some people, this was an invigorating milestone on the road to self-discovery; for others it was as scary as a bad trip on LSD. Relationships that had lasted years were wrecked for new experiments that often faded.

What's persisted, for many of us at least, has been the conviction that sexual expression is good—even better if two adults can enjoy it together without fear that they're auditioning for parenthood.

It's amazing, when you think of it, how quickly we've gotten used to this freedom. It suggests that the liberating dimension of sex is as natural a part of intimacy as procreation—and that being able to finally separate the two represents a real kind of progress, no matter how anxious that makes our more retrograde neighbors. Sex isn't just for procreation, nor is it merely, as porn would have it, another form of recreation. At its best it's a way for us to truly be ourselves with one another. That's why, if we're lucky, having sex is making love.

Talking about Pot:
That Unmentionable Object of Desire
February 24, 2010

Here's why changing the outdated marijuana laws in this country is taking longer than it should.

On February 1, a fifteen-second ad supporting the legalization of marijuana was supposed to start running on the giant CBS Super Screen billboard overlooking Times Square in New York City. The ad argued that taxing and regulating the sale of marijuana to adults would raise billions of dollars in new revenue.

The ad was created by the National Organization for the Reform of Marijuana Laws (NORML). A company called Neutron Media Screen Marketing, which manages the Times Square billboard for CBS, encouraged NORML to produce the spot and was prepared to play it eighteen times a day for two months.

On February 3, a Neutron Media representative sent this message to NORML headquarters: "I just received word from CBS and they will not approve your ad."

Now I am willing to bet that many of the people involved in this kind of decision-making at CBS have smoked marijuana, and not just once-upon-a-time in college, where they "experimented" with the stuff. Odds are that if you offered a toke to these folks, a fair number would indulge and thank you for the opportunity.

But few, if any, of them would admit it. And most of them would rather not have their corporation seen as appearing to countenance the idea that pot legalization might actually amount to worthwhile public policy.

When it comes to marijuana, most people deny their own experience with the stuff. They may smoke it, but the last thing they want to do is talk about it. The result is that it's taking much longer than it should for us to get a rational discussion going about how to clean up laws that have led to the arrest of twenty million people since 1965 and created a law enforcement bureaucracy that could certainly find better things to do with its time and resources.

It's not easy to conduct an open discussion of the potential benefits of an illegal substance. No one, especially those of us who are parents, wants to be perceived as a lawbreaker or, for that matter, irresponsible. So talk tends to duck and weave more than it should. We joke about getting high. We cite statistics. In the end, marijuana advocates wind up sounding like perpetual teenagers, forever arguing for their rights with older, supposedly wiser, elders.

Back in the 1960s, when smoking pot seemed more like a young person's rite of passage, this might have been understandable. In those days, the people warning about weed came packaged in ill-fitting dark suits, cut their grey hair short, and never, ever smiled, unless it was at someone else's expense. They used misinformation and cultural paranoia to make marijuana seem like an express bus to hell—and were easy targets for smart-ass satire.

Thankfully, these troglodytes are virtually extinct. But their laws and bogus mythologies remain. What's puzzling is that the mass of kids who came of age smoking pot, then went on to become successful lawyers, doctors, and business people, haven't done more to put those mythologies to rest.

In part, this may have something to do with the Baby Boom generation's love/hate relationship with its own experience. Sure, Boomers love to hear those golden oldies and watch endless shows about how they supposedly changed the world and the crazy things they did. But when it's come to turning their ideals into meaningful public policy, Boomers have flinched.

Boomers helped Ronald Reagan, a grandfather figure, become president in 1980, all but renouncing the social movements of the 1960s and '70s. It was a save-us-from-ourselves moment. And when Boomers finally chose one of their own, Bill Clinton, they tolerated his ridiculous claim of never having inhaled when he tried smoking pot in college.

Clinton's white lie about pot symbolized Boomers' middle-aged reluctance to challenge their parents' taboos—even when their own experience told them those taboos were laughably antique. It would be one thing if this reluctance were based in a genuine respect for older values. But, when it comes to marijuana laws, this is not the case. Many, if not most, Boomers have broken those laws again and again.

Some Boomers' reticence about coming out about pot is based on legitimate concerns about the health and safety of their kids and grandkids. They fear that legalizing pot would only make an already perilous world even more threatening. What, though, could be more dangerous than the unregulated black market, supplied by gangster cartels, that's making millions off pot today?

As long as pot exists in its current twilight zone, an unmentionable object of desire, illegal yet available, it will be difficult to move toward real reform of marijuana laws. The medical marijuana movement has created welcome pressure to think about pot in new, more realistic ways. But even it, finally, begs the ultimate question concerning what is gained by making this stuff illegal in the first place. It's not just the folks at CBS who need to come out of the closet about marijuana. Until pot smokers are willing to own their experiences with the herb, reform will languish.

Question Authority:
Sam Alito Didn't Get It

January 25, 2006

An awful lot was said during the confirmation hearings to determine Samuel Alito's qualifications for serving on the US Supreme Court. The transcripts from those proceedings will undoubtedly run to hundreds of pages. For me, though, the most interesting words spoken came on the very first day, when Alito made his opening statement. He was talking about what it was like to go to college, in his case Princeton, in the late 1960s and early 1970s. Here is what he said:

"It was a time of turmoil at colleges and universities. And I saw some very smart people and very privileged people behaving irresponsibly. And I couldn't help making a contrast between some of the worst of what I saw on the campus and the good sense and the decency of the people back in my community."

Alito delivered this recollection with complete confidence that the shorthand he was using to describe his college experience would be instantly grasped by his listeners. In a single stroke, he identified himself as a person who came of age during the 1960s and disavowed that period. Samuel Alito was not part of the "turmoil" that swept colleges and universities in those days. He, unlike the smart and privileged people he found himself among, was not irresponsible.

Alito was a member of the class of '72, which means that he started his college education in the fall of 1968. This was a particularly intense time to be on campus. The Vietnam War was raging. The previous spring and summer had been rocked by a series of traumatic events, including the murders of Martin Luther King and Robert Kennedy. There were race riots in American cities, including the burning of entire neighborhoods in Washington, DC. In August the Democratic National Convention in Chicago was upset when police attacked antiwar protesters in Grant Park, starting what was later declared a "police riot."

A year later, when Alito would have been in his second year on campus, it was revealed that the Nixon administration had been engaged in a secret bombing campaign in Cambodia. Student strikes and teach-ins took place on campuses across the country. There was a national march on Washington, and four students were shot and killed by National Guardsmen at Kent State University in Ohio.

That happened to be my freshman year. The college I attended in Minnesota ended classes early that spring because so many students were engaged in antiwar activities; it was as if a harsh wind had blown through our community and scattered many of us to the four corners of the nation.

It was a difficult and tumultuous time, to be sure. There were excesses on all sides. Hubert Humphrey, Lyndon Johnson's vice-president, was given a professorship at my school and, shortly after the first semester started, his office door was sealed shut with barbed wire by some students I knew. This may be the sort of thing Alito referred to as "behaving irresponsibly." At the time, though, rude as it may have been, it also seemed like a theatrically apt way for people with no power (and the prospect of having their draft numbers called) to put their anger in the face of one of the war's most prominent apologists. To his credit, Humphrey seemed to take it in stride.

Which is more than we can say for a lot of people. When he glibly summed up the upheavals of the late '60s and early '70s as a period of social irresponsibility, Samuel Alito spoke in favor of a version of America's history that's become a kind of conventional wisdom. Arguably the single largest project undertaken by the right wing in this country has been the demonization of virtually everything that happened here between the birth of Lyndon Johnson's Great Society programs in 1964 and the election of Ronald Reagan. According to this version of events, the country went to hell in a handbasket during this time. Then Reagan came along and saved us from ourselves.

A lot of regular folks who you would think might know better have bought this line. Maybe they got into trouble or hurt themselves with drugs or sex. Or perhaps they strayed from the high expectations for career and material success their parents instilled in them, only to panic later when they found themselves broke or somehow unfulfilled. In any event, these people were probably nodding in agreement when they heard Alito characterize his college days. Apart from a few Golden Oldies, that time is better off gone and forgotten as far as they're concerned.

Samuel Alito was playing to this crowd in his opening statement to the Senate Judiciary Committee. To them, he probably sounded reasonable. But I remember something besides bad behavior about that time he so briefly alluded to. The first principle of those days boiled down to just two words: question authority. That was a good idea then, when a president was waging an undeclared war overseas and illegally spying on Americans here at home. It's still a good idea. Unfortunately, I'm afraid that Samuel Alito didn't get it in the old days—and he doesn't get it now.

Tyranny of the Gun:
The Gun Owners Have Won
May 14, 2008

Ok, I get it now. I really do.

There's nothing we can do about guns.

Never mind that a little over a week ago somebody shot up a car down the block from where I live. Little chunks of glass are still lying in the street, like bits of toxic confetti.

But I understand: guns are not to blame.

I picked up the newspaper on Election Day. Here's what I found in the local news section: a seventeen-year-old boy was arrested in connection with the shooting death of another teen on the

Near Northside; a forty-nine-year-old man was charged with murder after shooting a man in the 3600 block of Arthington Boulevard; a man was shot and killed at Thirty-Eighth and Gale; and another teenager was fatally shot before crashing his car at Thirty-Fifth and Keystone.

As of the day I am writing this column, there have been forty homicides in Indianapolis; thirty of them have been shootings.

But guns are not the issue.

I have to admit that for a long time I believed that the way we treat and think about guns in this country was crazy. They're cheap and easy to get, and we practically encourage people to own them. And as those recent homicide statistics show, guns are also involved in a disproportionate amount of violent crimes, especially those that end with somebody being killed.

This, I used to think, represented a pattern, a kind of common denominator. If we could control guns or, at least, make them harder to come by, it stood to reason that fewer people would be getting shot.

I'm over that kind of thinking now.

It's not that I think guns have stopped being an antisocial danger, especially in cities where people, many of whom are unhappy, are in each other's faces a lot of the time. No, it's because it has become clear to me that the gun industry, gun owners, and the gun lobby have won.

This is how the mayor of Chicago, Richard Daley, put it not long ago. Almost thirty public school students, by the way, have been killed by guns in his city so far this year. "I firmly believe the gun industry is bigger than all the governments combined. It's the only institution that is fully protected by federal law, that you cannot sue them or you can't even question them. You look at the power of the gun industry—it is enormous in the United States…"

Daley is right. Just look at what's happening here in Indianapolis. We have a new mayor, Greg Ballard, who says fighting crime is his top priority. Ballard, in turn, appointed Scott Newman, a man with a reputation for being tough, chief of public safety. Although gun violence in the city continues, neither man has seen fit to so much as mention that guns might be part of the problem.

So you won't hear me calling for more gun control. You won't hear me questioning anybody's reading of the Second Amendment. Gun owners, you can take a deep breath because nobody here, least of all me, is going to pry anything away from you.

But here's the deal: since you're in charge, it would be nice to see you take a little responsibility. That put-upon, "everybody's trying to take away our guns" act is stale. It's high time that gun owners and businesses, as the beneficiaries of constitutional protection and lobbying muscle, took the lead in coming up with initiatives to fight crime in high-risk neighborhoods.

And I don't mean handing out flyers promoting gun safety or, worse, telling everyone to buy a gun so they can take the law into their own hands. This is the moral equivalent of Marie Antoinette telling her starving people to eat cake.

Marie Antoinette, of course, was a tyrant. As queen of France, she had the power to make things better for her country's people, but she was clueless and cut off from reality. She wanted to believe that her behavior affected no one but herself when, in fact, multitudes depended on her. In the end, they cut off her head.

Guns have created a tyranny of fear in neighborhoods through-out this city. It is clear, though, that doing anything to regulate or control guns is the last thing on the minds of the powers-that-be. Gun owners and advocates need to be accountable for the power they command. It's their world—so far, the rest of us are just living in it.

David Hoppe

Guns Win the Martin Case:
Enabling American Paranoia
July 24, 2013

There were plenty of losers in the Trayvon Martin case. From Martin's parents, who forever lost their son, to the American jury system, which took a severe hit to its credibility, the field was strewn with bodies, not the least being Martin himself, shot and killed at the age of seventeen.

Even George Zimmerman, the shooter acquitted in Martin's killing, is not unscathed. He walked out of the courtroom a marked man.

The only winner in this rash and violent story is America's paranoid crush on guns.

We like to call America the land of the free. But there has always been a great fear beneath the surface of this boast. "Freedom is not free," says a popular bumper sticker, meaning not just that we have to work at liberty, but be prepared to defend it from a world that apparently lives for nothing so much as to take our freedom away.

That world is a dangerous place.

This message took hold from the time the first colonists arrived on the shores of what was a wild and scary land. Nature was experienced as a predatory force. Everything from the weather to the people already living here was seen as being out to get us. Survival meant a fight.

We've never lost this attitude. Many would say it's been the secret of our success. As an old Confederate cavalry general, Nathan Bedford Forrest, anticipating the doctrine of shock and awe by over a century, once said, the secret to winning a fight is "to get there firstest with the mostest."

That's why George Zimmerman, a Florida neighborhood watch volunteer, brought his gun on the night he followed Trayvon

Martin. A rash of burglaries and vandalism in his neighborhood had prompted Zimmerman to start a neighborhood watch group. People there were on edge. As one woman, whose house was broken into, told Amy Green for the *Daily Beast*, "There was definitely a sense of fear in the neighborhood after all of this started happening, and it just kept on happening. It wasn't just a one-time thing. It was every week…Our next-door neighbor actually said if someone came into his yard he would shoot him. If someone came into his house he would shoot him. Everyone felt afraid and scared."

The sense in the neighborhood was that young black men were the perpetrators. Trayvon Martin, as they say, fit that profile.

But Martin wasn't doing anything illegal. He was a kid, visiting his dad.

George Zimmerman was carrying a gun. When Zimmerman saw Martin, he called the police. The dispatcher said, "Are you following him?"

"Yeah," replied Zimmerman.

Dispatcher: "OK, we don't need you to do that."

As we know, Zimmerman did it anyway. He got there firstest with the mostest, and, a few minutes later, Trayvon Martin was dead.

Being afraid is a horrible thing. I once lived in a house that police told us was targeted by a burglary gang. Black teens knocked on our door at various times of the day and night to see when and whether we were home. The cops told us this gang would surely break in and that we should call for help as soon as they did, but that they—the police—couldn't do anything until that moment.

This made me furious, as well as afraid. I could have bought a gun, played an American urban pioneer. I could have turned out like George Zimmerman. I moved instead.

Not everyone can do that. That's one reason gun sales keep climbing.

This ascent has been given a boost by the law called "Stand Your Ground." A collaboration between the corporate-funded American Legislative Exchange Council (ALEC) and the National Rifle Association (NRA), this legislation enables public paranoia in the cause of self-defense. It legalizes the use of deadly force if a person (according to the law), "reasonably believes it is necessary to do so to prevent death or great bodily harm to himself or herself or another, or to prevent the commission of a forcible felony."

The NRA carried this so-called model bill to the Florida legislature, where it was passed in 2005. Since then the ALEC model has been adopted by sixteen states, including Wisconsin, where on March 3, a twenty-year-old college student, also black, named Bo Morrison was shot and killed by a homeowner in the town of Slinger. Morrison was hiding in some bushes, trying to evade police after attending an underage drinking party.

Fear has been a tonic for the gun business. Guns are a twelve-billion-dollar-a-year industry in this country. In 2005, the same year that the NRA and ALEC got their model bill passed in Florida, Congress passed an NRA-lobbied law granting gunmakers immunity from liability lawsuits related to gun violence in American cities. Clearly, the gun is our drug of choice for dealing with whatever, and whoever, scares us.

George Zimmerman followed his fear the night he killed Trayvon Martin. Given that fear, he probably thought it was smart to be carrying a gun. What happened next was justified by a law and backed by an entire industry. Most of all, it was fed by paranoia: America's national pastime.

Our Specialty Is War: We're Hooked
February 10, 2010

It's been widely observed that awarding the Nobel Peace Prize to President Barack Obama had more to do with wishful thinking than accomplishment. Obama himself said as much.

On reflection, though, the prize may have had less to do with Obama than with those of us who voted for him. Obama was a surrogate. What the Nobel committee was really doing was sending a message to American voters. They wanted to thank us for electing a guy who seemed to think this country was something more than the world's biggest war machine.

Apparently the folks in Oslo are unfamiliar with addiction. They grossly underestimated the depth of our jones for shock and awe.

We like to call this our Defense Budget. That's like calling a street gang a youth organization, but never mind. Here's what the newly minted Nobel laureate has proposed to spend on our military in fiscal year 2011: $708 billion. Add an additional $33 billion the Obama administration has asked Congress to approve as an "emergency supplemental," and the total comes to $741 billion.

This has been called the largest military budget (adjusted for inflation) since World War II. Others have pointed out that this means our government will be spending over $2 billion per day on war.

The announcement of this spending plan was good news for the socialist sector of our economy: those corporations that live to make things the government pays for. Harris Corp, which specializes in radio encryption technology, saw its stock rise 4.2 percent. At General Dynamics, where they manufacture munitions, submarines, and warplanes, shares went up 3.9 percent. Northrop Grumman, maker of unmanned spy planes, rose 2.3 percent. Pity poor Raytheon, the missile maker. Its shares only jumped a single percentage point.

The USA is responsible for 41.5 percent of total world military spending. In second place is China; they account for 5.8 percent. France is third at 4.5 percent. No one, in other words, comes close to us when it comes to "defense."

Addicts, we know, will come up with any number of reasons to justify their all-consuming habits. They'll say their drug of choice makes them feel more alive, that it kills their pain or, simply, that it makes it possible for them to function. Finally, though, the drug, whatever it is, becomes its own reason. You plan your days around it because there's nothing else to do. You may do other things, but a junkie is what you are.

Making war is the American drug of choice. Almost 45 percent of our tax dollars go to military spending and the cost of past wars. Meanwhile we argue about budget deficits and whether or not we can afford to pay for health care (19.7 percent of tax dollars), respond to poverty (11.8 percent), or provide a better educational system (2.2 percent).

Policy makers, including Obama, who want to freeze nonmilitary expenditures, will say we're spending enough on education; we just need to spend it better. No one says this about the military.

That's because, like any powerful drug, the military has consumed us. Indiana is a good example. We hear all the time about the blows to our once-proud manufacturing sector. But guess what part of Indiana manufacturing is booming right now. In an excellent 2008 series in Fort Wayne's *Journal Gazette*, Dan Stockman researched the extent to which military spending props up Indiana's economy. He reported that in 2006, the federal government spent $6.05 billion on defense in Indiana, making it a bigger part of our economy than farming, which brought in $5.97 billion. According to Stockman's findings, defense spending in Indiana totaled $960 for every Hoosier man, woman, and child.

Stockman underlined our dependence on military spending in terms of jobs. In July 2008 unemployment was 6.5 percent in the Fort Wayne area. That figure would have been almost 10 percent without those tax-supported, defense-related jobs.

The next time someone tells you they don't want government-run health care, ask them why health care should be held to a different standard than the makers of bombs and flak jackets.

Functioning addicts are expert at keeping up appearances. They get to work on time and pay the proper respects. It's like the way our war-addled country insists on reserving a special day for Dr. Martin Luther King, Jr. Dr. King said, "When a nation becomes obsessed with the guns of war, social programs must inevitably suffer. We can talk about guns and butter all we want to, but when the guns are there with all its emphasis, you don't even get good oleo. These are facts of life."

It wasn't that long ago that President Obama called for sending thirty thousand more troops to fight in Afghanistan. Evidently this is his idea of a jobs program. But this is what happens in an age of specialization. It just so happens that America's specialty is war.

The Unmaking of the President: Obama, the Unboss
January 9, 2012

In early 2008, when Barack Obama was running for president, some of his critics took pleasure in pointing out that the young senator from Illinois hailed from Chicago, a city known for its "machine" brand of politics. Obama, they suggested, owed his rapid rise through the Democratic ranks to connections with the city's mayor, Richard M. Daley, son of a previous Chicago mayor, the legendary Richard J. Daley, also known as hizzoner or, as another Chicago legend, the journalist Mike Royko, put it, Boss.

Over the holidays, I read Royko's 1971 takedown of the elder Daley, *Boss: Richard J. Daley of Chicago*. Published when Daley was entering the sixteenth of what would finally be twenty-one years in office, Royko's book is a relentlessly focused attack on Daley's reputation as a mayor who made Chicago, as signs on its borders proudly proclaimed, "the city that works."

Royko doesn't deny Daley's accomplishments. As he points out, they are plainly visible for all to see: Chicago's downtown, the Loop, was revitalized and its skyline reinvented; a vast network of expressways connected all parts of the city and suburbs; a new air-

David Hoppe

port, O'Hare, connected Chicago with the rest of the country and the world.

But this juggernaut of progress had a cost. As Royko observes, "Behind the high-rises are the crumbling, crowded buildings where the lower-income people live. No answer has been found to their housing problems because the real estate people say there's not enough profit in building homes for them. And beyond them are the middle-income people, who can't make it to the high-rises and can't stay where they are because the schools are inadequate, the poor are pushing toward them, and nothing is being done about their problems, so they move to the suburbs. When their children grow up and they retire, maybe then they can move to a lake front high-rise."

As Royko makes clear, Daley was able to get big things done in Chicago by keeping a vise-like grip on power, what Chicagoans came to call "clout." Daley ruled the city as a despot, which meant that things got done without the niceties of democratic process. In Chicago connections and payoffs were a part of doing business. Contractors were enriched, people were put to work, and Daley kept it running by maintaining a steely discipline, often enforced by his police department, which operated in a kind of extra-legal zone.

Reading *Boss* today, one is outraged by Daley's egregious treatment of racial minorities, the disadvantaged, and anybody else who didn't advance his bare-knuckle agenda. But Royko's book also raises bigger, enduring questions about democratic governance. What would Chicago have been like if instead of command decisions, every building project would have been subject to rounds of community meetings and a conscientious process aimed at consensus?

Would there be an O'Hare Field? It was built in spite of people's concerns about noise and traffic congestion. A John Hancock skyscraper? Planners and architecture buffs argued such a big building would ruin the neighborhood's historic character. Or, for that matter, a Picasso on the city's Civic Center Plaza? The public thought a statue of baseball player Ernie Banks made more sense.

Fast forward to 2012. We are faced with a clutch of big-picture issues, from implementing strategies to save the planet to providing universal health care and viable forms of public transportation. We know these things are important. But a power outage at the top keeps them in a state of perpetual stalemate, subject to the me-first whims of special interests and squeaky wheels. Without clout, democracy has a way of chasing its tail.

That's how things have gone since President Obama took office. He said he was going to change the way things were done in Washington. He called for a new era of civility, for bipartisanship, when what he really needed was more old-fashioned clout.

It's turned out that whether he's dealing with health care reform, the economy, or global warming, Obama lacks the political will, the real power, or both, to govern effectively. Not even making Boss Daley's son, William, his chief of staff, in place of current Chicago mayor Rahm Emanuel, has helped.

Which makes Obama's New Year's Eve signing of the National Defense Authorization Act, a law that makes United States citizens subject to arrest and indefinite detention by the military, more than a little ironic. The Obama administration has said it would never take full advantage of this law but, as the American Civil Liberties Union has pointed out, the law has "no temporal or geographic limitations." Meaning a President Romney, let's say, could find the law's open-ended language a handy way of disappearing someone who was particularly annoying (mind your manners, Newt Gingrich!).

When this law was originally presented to Obama, he said he wouldn't sign it. Then a bipartisan group of senators, including McCain, Liebermann, and Webb, pressed the issue, and Obama backed down. Again.

Obama's now accused of grabbing power when it appears as likely he merely caved to pressure. This supposedly made man from Chicago must have old man Daley rolling in his grave.

Hiding behind the First Amendment: Media Violence Is Pollution
May 2, 2007

A couple of weeks ago, when Mayor Peterson held a press conference to raise concerns about the impact of media violence on children, I showed up early. I wasn't the first one there; a couple of guys were already on the scene, and I overheard them talking about the subject at hand. Their conversation went something like this:

"You know," one of the guys was saying with the kind of overwhelming self-assurance guys sometimes assume when they want you to know they've been around the block a few times, watched a heckuvalot of TV, seen *Hostel* and all the *Saw* movies, not to mention all those hours playing *Grand Theft Auto*, "no matter how they try to cut it, the research doesn't add up. They can't show a causal connection between what people watch and what they do."

The guy he was talking to furrowed his brow and nodded. He allowed that research was a good thing, but that people needed to remember this was also a free speech issue.

I was suddenly overcome with déjà vu. I had heard these sorts of exchanges before, back in those not-so-distant days when "experts" in the media kept telling us the jury was still out on the effects of human behavior on climate change, that more studies were needed before we could take action.

I realize that in some quarters we're still hearing that today. And Dick Cheney is still insisting that Saddam had weapons of mass destruction.

Anyway, the mayor arrived. He brought a number of people with him, including a former commissioner from the Federal Communications Commission, a psychologist, a family advocate, a representative of the video games industry and, last but not least, a mom. The mayor, we know, has had a checkered history trying to deal with violent video games. As he explained to us, the Columbine massacre deeply affected him. It made him keenly aware of the extent to which our society glorifies violence, and he wants to do something about that. One of the first things he tried was to regulate the availability of violent video games to youth in Indianapolis. This was struck down by the courts.

While now conceding that regulating this kind of material "isn't going to fly," Mayor Peterson, who is watching his city suffer a crime wave at the moment, hasn't given up on trying to deal with our culture's propensity for violence. He wants people to be thinking about it and talking about it. He wants the media to take greater responsibility for the images of violent behavior and exploitation that it relies on to pad its bottom line.

As the mayor spoke, I sensed a tension in the room. That tension wasn't about kids or crime; it was about money. "We all want the same things," he said, referring to his guests and, more specifically, to the people representing the video game industry. "We just differ on how to get there."

Nobody is for murder, beating women, or child abuse. But media producers derive big profits by depicting these behaviors, packaging them and making them available, at all hours, via an ever-growing array of delivery systems. They know that as offensive as these images are, there's something in the human animal that wants to look—and that we'll pay for the chance.

There's a lot of money to be made in spewing this stuff. Media producers want to make that money as long as they can; they don't want to stop. When they suspect that someone might hold them accountable—draw a line between the permission for antisocial behavior their images suggest and violent acts in the real world, they take cover behind the First Amendment—as if the freedom of speech was really a license to print money.

The psychologist the mayor brought to his press conference was careful to say that it was almost impossible to find a causal connection between media products and particular acts of violence. But she emphasized that there was no question about violent media being a risk factor affecting the development of kids. In a way it was like saying that while we can't blame our heavy use of fossil fuels on that terrible cold spell we had last February, we can safely say that if we keep polluting the atmosphere, there's going to be hell to pay.

Just as we're finding that the real price of petroleum must include all the costs associated with what it does to our health and the environment, we need to find a way to make the producers of violent media take responsibility for what they're doing to our cultural environment. Violent media is like gasoline: just because we get off on it doesn't mean it's good for us. We don't need more research to know this; we need common sense.

Around the Campfire on the Digital Age: Watching TV with My Son
June 13, 2007

Our son is home from college. There is music playing on the stereo that I've never heard before, and shoes, big ones, lying here and there in a kind of trail leading from the front door to the family room. It's all good: in our household, our son's arrival has come to signify the official beginning of summer.

Our son has blessed us in many ways, not the least of which happens to be his penchant for watching TV. This, I admit, he probably inherited from me. I thoroughly enjoy watching TV, even when I know that what I'm watching is a waste of, among other things, time. There's something perversely luxurious about this. Yes, sometimes taking the time to watch an old sitcom feels like the equivalent of lighting a hand-rolled cigar with a hundred-dollar bill.

The problem is that I'm a creature of habit. When it comes to

TV I know what I like: a B-movie on TCM, say, or another misspent afternoon watching the Cubs blow a lead in the late innings. I tend to stick with the tried and true.

My son, on the other hand, likes to graze. When he's around, my viewing horizon gets a good stretching. I doubt, for example, that I would have experienced the surgically enhanced cavalcade that was this year's Miss Universe pageant, complete with Miss USA's unscripted pratfall during the evening gown competition, had it not been for my wisecracking son.

The other night the two of us were watching something—another riotous episode of Prime Minister's Question Time on C-SPAN, I think—and my son remarked that our old TV had held up pretty well over the years. This is true: as best we could recollect, we bought the thing when he was in middle school. But, I told him, the time was drawing nigh when we would have to junk it. In less than two years, in February 2009, an act of Congress will render our trusty analog set obsolete.

After years of hemming and hawing, Congress finally decided that on February 18, 2009, TV stations will switch entirely to digital programming, or HDTV. People say it will be the biggest change in video technology since the introduction of color TV in the 1950s. While this doesn't mean that all of us with analog TVs will have to throw our sets away—your analog set can receive digital signals through the use of a converter box—it appears many folks are already using the deadline as an excuse to go out and upgrade their sets, leading to concern that millions and millions of old TVs will wind up in the trash. "There's going to be an e-waste tsunami that hits America," John Shegerian, chief executive of Electronic Recyclers in Fresno, California, told the *Los Angeles Times*.

But never mind about that. If you're going to make an omelet, you have to break a few cathode ray tubes. The point is that, with very little public discussion or media coverage, the government is about to reach into every one of our homes and mess with what many Americans probably consider the most important appliance they possess: their television. According to the latest US census, the average household has 2.5 of 'em. In all, there are 268 million TVs from sea to shining sea.

Some might consider this a great intrusion on the government's part. Others, though, might see it as an example of America's can-do spirit. Here was an old technology standing in the way of a new, better technology. I mean, think of it: Who would rather have Oprah in 640x480 pixels when you could have her in 1,920x1,080?

That this conversion is for our own good should be obvious. And for those who worry that some among us might not be able to afford a new HDTV set, don't. The government has actually set aside several billion dollars to buy converter boxes so that people like me can bring my analog TV up to digital speed. "We take the position that, if we're mandating this conversion, we cannot leave people behind," said Alaska's magnanimous Senator Ted Stevens.

It's amazing what our government can accomplish when it sees a problem and determines to solve it. The resolution may not be popular with everyone, and it may cause some headaches along the way, but that's the price you pay for progress.

My son said it made him wonder. If we can do this with our TVs, why not with our cars—mandate that every vehicle on the road gets 45 mpg—or our health care—guarantee that everyone has coverage, regardless of their ability to pay. And while we're at it, why can't we declare that we'll begin to seriously invest in alternative forms of energy, like wind and solar power?

The Cubs are playing, I said. The game's just begun.

The Cubs and Crocuses: Hope Springs Eternal
March 17, 2010

It's March, and although they're still shuddering on El platforms in Chicago and expecting a late blizzard in Minneapolis, here in Indy, crocuses are blooming.

Whatever else you might say about this town, our spring starts on time.

There's a fundamental rightness about the fact that our first flowers begin appearing when baseball players start playing practice games in Florida and Arizona. For me, these things go together like a rhyming couplet about how hope springs eternal.

This is especially true if, like me, you have lived your life following one baseball team in particular: the Chicago Cubs.

I was hooked not long after I learned to walk. Amazingly enough, I have a vivid memory of the very moment my fate was sealed. My dad had just returned from the drugstore, where he'd gone to get a Sunday paper. But, in addition to the newspaper, he'd also purchased a pack of baseball cards. I remember standing by our front door as Dad peeled open the waxy paper that contained the cards and the knowledgeable, man-to-man way he murmured to me about the pros and cons of the players who were ritualistically pictured gripping bats or extending their mitts.

We were almost to the bottom of this little deck when Dad's tone suddenly brightened. In my little fist was a picture of a young player with his arms held up over his head in an almost Kabuki-style approximation of a wind-up. He wore a blue cap with a red C on the front and, across his chest, was a code I would soon learn to unscramble: C-H-I-C-A-G-O.

"You got a Cub!" Dad exclaimed. "That's great!"

Apart from certain virulent strains of influenza, it's hard to think of anything in life as infectious as enthusiasm. At this moment, that baseball card was like a conductor carrying a charge of enthusiasm straight from my dad to me.

The player's name was Don Kaiser. He turned out to be an undistinguished pitcher on a terrible team. But on that Sunday morning in our living room, he was a star. Dad briefly perused the back of Don Kaiser's baseball card to see what, if anything, might recommend him. Finding little to go on, Dad resorted to the default mode I would learn was a refuge for Cubs fans going back to 1908: "He's a good guy," said Dad. "The Cubs are good guys."

Nineteen-ought-eight was the last time the Cubs won the World Series. That's 102 years without winning the big one, the longest running exercise in futility—or quest, as some of us prefer to think of it—in American professional sports.

Needless to say, Dad was a lifelong Cubs fan. He caught the bug from his dad. They lived in Sauganash, a residential neighborhood on Chicago's north side. In those days, professional baseball players walked among us mortals. A Cubs pitcher lived across the street, and, on a occasion, the players partied there. Dad still remembers "Jolly Cholly" Grimm, the first baseman and manager, reclining on the hood of a parked car, playing the banjo and singing for the kids.

That was the 1930s. The Cubs fielded good teams in those years, just not good enough to win the World Series. And they haven't made it that far since 1945. If you'd asked my Dad—or any other Cubs fan—in 1945 if they thought it would be over sixty years and counting before they'd see the Cubs back on top of the National League, they would have said something like, "Sure, and someday a B-movie actor like Ronald Reagan will be president!"

Cubs fans have had to find ways to cope with this ongoing drought that tap deep into our psyches. There's something existential about it. Bill Murray said it best after the team imploded during the 2003 playoffs. According to Murray, Cubs fans had lived through losing before and knew how to deal with it. "We are not like the others," he said.

So the biggest news coming out of spring training this year has revolved around a former Cub, the perpetually disgruntled Milton Bradley. After being signed to a three-year, $30 million deal, Bradley proceeded to have an awful year for the Cubs in 2009. He responded to his inability to perform by blaming Cubs fans, the team, even the city itself. He said he was the target of racial slurs. The team suspended Bradley at the end of the season and dumped him over the winter.

The Cubs apparently thought signing Bradley would bring the team some missing "attitude." This backfired, to say the least. Bradley only reinforced what we've known all along: to be a Cub, like my Dad said, you must be a good guy. Not, in other words, like the others.

In Arizona, where the Cubs are training, everyone, even the cynics who cover the team for a living, talk about how good-natured the clubhouse has become. And in Indianapolis, the crocuses are blooming.

Crossing Oprah: Facts vs. Truth
February 8, 2006

An old friend of mine, let's call him Jack, is a marvelous storyteller. Years ago, when I first met Jack, I was enchanted by some of the stories he told about his exploits in New York and Los Angeles during the 1950s and '60s. These stories, often told at dinner parties, were colorful, loaded with incident and famous names. They were also instructive. Jack was not a braggart. His best stories were usually told by way of illustrating a larger point about dealing with disappointment, say, or talent, or success.

Jack taught me many things, one being that it was a good idea to take his stories with a grain of salt. The better I got to know him, the more clear it became that Jack's stories weren't always informed by a literal adherence to the facts. He embroidered. He embellished.

I learned that when it came to many of his best stories, an old line applied: if they weren't true, they should have been.

That Jack might have played it fast and loose with the facts didn't make him a bad guy as far as I was concerned. His stories didn't hurt anybody. And besides, they were great entertainment—vivid and even edifying. If parts of them were made up or exaggerated, well, the only disappointment was finding that Jack, apart from his gift of gab, was pretty much like the rest of us.

I've been thinking about Jack lately in light of the brouhaha that's arisen concerning James Frey's bestselling book, *A Million Little Pieces*, and his public chastisement by his former patron and advocate, Oprah Winfrey. Frey's is a redemptive story about drug addiction and self-destruction and how, in the end, he turns his life around. The book, which Frey and his agent originally called a novel, was rejected by a string of publishers. Then they decided to call it a memoir, and it was snapped up by Nan A. Talese, an imprint of Random House. There are now three million copies of *A Million Little Pieces* in print in North America, in large part thanks to Oprah making it her book club selection for October 2005. Oprah, it seems, loves stories about people who pull themselves together, and her legion of viewers love what Oprah loves. Thus Oprah's book club has become a major force in American publishing.

But shortly after Oprah endorsed *A Million Little Pieces*, stories surfaced that debunked some of what passed for facts in Frey's narrative. For some reason, this powerful story didn't seem so powerful if it wasn't true. Frey was interviewed by Larry King, who challenged the veracity of his tale. "I think of this book working in the long tradition of Hemingway and Kerouac and Bukowski," said Frey, citing novelists famously known for disguising autobiography as fiction, rather than the other way around.

The highlight of the King show came when Oprah herself called in. While allowing that maybe some facts in the story didn't add up, Oprah said, "The underlying message of redemption in James Frey's memoir still resonates with me."

At this point, Oprah was sounding like an artist. She was willing to make a distinction that makes art possible: that is, to recognize that facts don't necessarily add up to truth. The facts in Frey's story may not add up, but the power of that story moved Oprah and, she claimed, a lot of other people, too.

Trouble is, we live in a literalistic world, a world not given to metaphor or the strategies of art. This is a world that confuses art and advertising, where expression is less important than persuasion and a story's only good if it makes you do what it wants you to. What's more, ours is a celebrity culture that values personalities over the work they do.

Oprah's willingness to cut Frey some slack in favor of what she thought was his story's larger truth got her in trouble. As far as the American media establishment was concerned, she was defending a liar. Never mind that they've been doing the same thing with George Bush over war in Iraq where people are being killed. Oprah would have to make amends.

So she called Frey and his publisher on to her show and reamed them both. The *Chicago Tribune* covered the confrontation on its front page. Columnists across the country celebrated the scourging. Diane Sawyer, fellow TV star and former Nixon aide, gushed, "It was a master class in bravery. [Oprah] reminded everyone of the power of telling the truth."

In fact, what she did was to show us that a guy named James Frey is less interesting than we might have thought, and that the feelings we might formerly have had for the story he told were…what? Last week, in a fit of literalistic pique, a California woman named Karen Futernick sued Random House for $50 million. "Nobody can get away with profiting with a product that you represented as something that it is not," fumed her lawyer.

I feel sorry for Jack. He may never be invited to dinner again.

God Save the Queen:
Before It's Too Late
May 16, 2007

I made a point of watching Queen Elizabeth on her recent trip to the States. McCartney was right: though she doesn't have a lot to say, Liz seems like a pretty nice girl. And those hats! Every day a new bonnet in some color derived from a wildflower cited in a Shakespeare play.

We Americans have mixed feelings about royalty. Having rejected the idea in a fit of youthful bravado back in 1776, a certain part of us retains a wistfulness for monarchy. Our being constitutionally opposed to the concept hasn't kept us from creating surrogates, called celebrities, whose actual accomplishments, like Elizabeth's, are unspecifiable, but whose tastes and foibles—like the love of small dogs, big houses, and sporting events—provide constant fodder for magazines, talk shows and twenty-four-hour news.

To tell you the truth, I think the time is coming when we'll find that a queen, or king—a supreme leader, if you prefer—could come in handy. How else are we going to deal with climate change?

Let me tell you what I mean. The other night I was watching the weather forecast on TV. The North American continent was covered with animated swooshes of citrus color, tangerine, lemon, and lime, indicating warm Pacific air originating somewhere south of the equator. The weatherman, an affable fellow approved by the American Meteorological Society, said that his colleagues had spotted activity out there over the South Seas suggesting that the summer to come could bring an unusually long string of ninety-degree days.

The next day, on my way home from work, I noticed the temperature was 85. And it wasn't even the middle of May. Through my open upstairs windows I could hear the air conditioning kick in at my next-door neighbor's house.

Here's my point: many, maybe even most, of us understand the importance of cutting down on greenhouse gases. We see stories almost every day about scientists warning us that time is running out before we reach the point of no return in terms of avoiding the worst effects of rising temperatures. Turn around and someone else is talking about the ice melting in Greenland.

Meanwhile, we dutifully collect our recyclables, ride our bikes, and screw in those twirly lightbulbs that are supposed to outlive many small mammals. But tell me: How many of us will be willing to forego the unspeakable bliss of an air-conditioned workplace in the midst of a prolonged heat wave?

I happen to work on the upper floor of a building that, in a fit of late twentieth-century technological optimism, was designed with windows that cannot be opened. Even on a sunny winter day it can get overheated. If we have a prolonged heat wave this summer, I can guarantee you that the AC here, and in every building similarly equipped, will be chugging.

In his book about life in Washington, DC, during World War II, David Brinkley pointed out that foreign diplomats used to hate being sent to our nation's capital; it was unbearably hot and humid, considered a hardship post. Then came air conditioning and every-thing changed. People could work all day and party all night in cool comfort.

Well, the climate in Washington, DC, is remarkably similar to that of Indianapolis. And we're just as hooked on AC. Our workdays, indeed, our very understanding of time and motion, are scheduled as if weather doesn't exist. Not long ago our public schools made a big deal out of putting AC in every building so that kids' time in class could be extended. This was supposed to be good news. If we have a string of ninety-degree days, the dominant sound in every neighbor-hood here will be the whir and gurgle of energy-chomping cooling systems. Just try telling people to live without.

That's why I think we need a queen—or king. And not some milk-and-cookies monarch, either, someone with teeth. If scientists from the Intergovernmental Panel on Climate Change, an organization sponsored by the United Nations (whose findings, by the way, are supported by the Bush administration) are correct, we have until 2015—eight years!—to get our act together. That will still leave billions of people short of water by 2050.

But in Detroit, automakers insist making cars that get more than twenty-seven miles of gas to the gallon isn't good for business. Air-polluting coal is still the fuel of choice in our cities. And who among us will leave the AC switched to "off" as the temperature outside rises this summer? At a certain point, freedom of choice just looks like dithering.

That's why we need a queen. Someone to make the decisions for us we're unable to make on our own.

History on Its Ear:
A New Book about UK Punk
May 7, 2008

History ain't what it used to be…

Thirty years ago, in 1978, the Institute of Contemporary Art in London presented a major exhibition to mark the fifteenth anniversary of the rock band, The Who. This was a big deal. No one had based a museum-quality art show on a rock band before. But even more mind-blowing was the idea that a band could last that long. In those days, fifteen years seemed like an eternity.

At least that's how the likes of Malcolm McLaren, John (Rotten) Lydon, Joe Strummer, and Mick Jones looked at things. As far as these progenitors of punk were concerned, bands like The Who belonged in a museum. The punks were insurgents, upstarts dedicated to liberating a scene corrupted by the power structure that had coalesced around the superstar bands of the '60s. Their story is briskly told in an entertaining new book about punk's moment, *Pretty Vacant: A History of UK Punk* by Phil Strongman (Chicago Review Press).

Strongman's story actually gets rolling in the States, as he outlines how bands like the Velvet Underground, MC5, the Stooges, and the New York Dolls set the stage for punk by deliberately flying in the face of the prevailing late '60s penchant for psychedelic narcissism and endless guitar solos. Eventually a scene would emerge in New York around the Mercer Arts Center and CBGBs, with bands like The Ramones, Blondie, Television, and Patti Smith.

I happened to be in London in 1976, when Smith played her first concert in the UK. I was hanging out at the National Poetry Centre and taking a fan's pride in turning people on to Smith's first album, *Horses*. This was a gas because as soon as people heard this record they went nuts with enthusiasm. And no wonder: in a musical landscape dominated by Fleetwood Mac and *Frampton Comes Alive*, Patti Smith was the sonic equivalent of the Heimlich maneuver.

The British music press didn't quite know what to make of Smith. In the days leading up to her show, there were articles intimating her sexuality wasn't quite right. One writer in the *New Musical Express* seemed put off by her androgynous image. But this didn't keep a huge crowd from showing up at the Roundhouse to see her.

Punk began being born that night. I'd never seen anything like the weird confederacy assembled there. Proto-punks, The Stranglers, opened with a hostile set designed to antagonize everybody. Then Smith and her band came out.

I wish I could say it was a great set, but Patti was out of it. She shambled about the stage, ran off at the mouth, and forgot the words to songs. The crowd, which had been in a fever to see her, grew restive, then strangely quiet. At one point, a woman yelled out, "We love you, Patti!" as if to try and will things back to coherence. It didn't work.

Strongman includes a photo of this wild-eyed debacle in his book. He also does a fine job of evoking the mood in London in that year before punk broke through. The city was hot and plagued with breakdowns, strikes, and impatience. The Labour government was on its last legs, and Margaret Thatcher, the "Iron Lady," was in the wings, about to make the punks' most paranoid dreams come true.

Thirty years later, punk rock lives on, its exhortation to Do It Yourself more relevant than ever. New technologies have put a recording studio in every laptop, and every band can be its own label. The result has been an ever-expanding musical universe in which history has ceased to be a progression of one Big Thing after another in favor of a continuous present in which everything is included and available.

A couple of weeks ago I was in Three Oaks, Michigan, to see a documentary film about Frank D'Rone, a seventy-something cabaret singer who has counted Frank Sinatra, Nat King Cole, and Tony Bennett among his biggest fans. Like those artists, D'Rone is a master of the classic American Songbook, a body of work that fell out of commercial favor through the 1970s and much of the '80s. D'Rone was in the wilderness for quite awhile.

But the other night D'Rone was beaming, with a new DVD, a web site, and an audience who thinks he's cool. Strangely enough, that's because thirty years ago the punks stood history on its ear.

Who's a Rock Star?
Mick Jagger, That's Who
April 30, 2013

"You're a rock star." People say this as a kind of shorthand describing someone's status. It doesn't mean you can play an instrument or carry a tune. It means you've got juice, mojo, something extra.

The funny thing about calling somebody a rock star is that they seem to be a dying breed. Take Mick Jagger, for example. If ever there was a guy to call a rock star, it'd have to be Mick. He practically invented the term.

Last week, Mick, along with his mates in the Rolling Stones, announced plans to embark on an abbreviated North American tour. They'll play arenas in nine cities; the closest the band will come to Indianapolis is Chicago's United Center, for three dates. Tickets for that show start at 85 bucks and run as high as $600. Prices like that, I guess, are what being a rock star is really about. But those prices also suggest the end of a particular line.

The Rolling Stones have been together through fifty summers. Their drummer, Charlie Watts, is seventy-one years old. Mick—SIR Mick, now—will turn seventy in July, a month after the band headlines the Glastonbury Festival. His Glimmer Twin, Keith Richards, reaches the big 7-0 in time for this coming Christmas. While some have rightly pointed out that this graying version of the Stones is simply following in the footsteps of their seemingly ageless blues mentors, all of whom played until they dropped, this doesn't quite get at the whole of what this septuagenarian Stones spectacle means.

It's worth remembering that the Rolling Stones started out as an almost academic project: skinny English white boys fervently studying and then trying their best to perform like the black American blues giants they idolized. Their name was an homage to a Muddy Waters song, and they went so far as to record their first number-one hit at the Chess studio in Chicago where Waters and other bluesmen worked.

The Stones arrived in the States in the '60s as part of the Beatles-inspired British Invasion. At first, the band tried to set itself apart by being the anti-Beatles, a group that meant to bite your hand instead of hold it. They made the most of bad publicity, publicly pissing on walls and being caught in titillating situations with drugs and girlfriends.

But it wasn't until the Beatles' break-up that the Stones found their immediately identifiable sound, the aural equivalent of a flick knife in a boxing glove. Between their 1969 recording of the darkly prophetic "Gimme Shelter" and the truly murderous shambles of their concert in December of that year at Altamont, California, where tripping hippies were bludgeoned in front of the stage by Hell's Angels, the Stones almost singlehandedly brought down the curtain on the self-proclaimed decade of peace and love.

It's hard, at this historical remove, to grasp how important these things felt at the time. Counterculture, although not broadly embraced, was nevertheless gaining traction—not only in teenage bedrooms, but on campuses, creative businesses, and even in some outposts in Vietnam. Rock music was at the heart of this movement, and the people who played it weren't seen as just musicians; they were treated like shamans, whose influence could seem to transcend that of most politicians or, for that matter, any other class of public figure.

The rock star idea was born. Mick Jagger and the Rolling Stones made the most of it. By the 1970s, the Stones had figured out how to infuse the blues' darkest veins with that decade's sexual privateering and political dissolution. They were one hell of a dance band; at their best they could scare you and turn you on at the same time.

A lot of blood has washed under the bridge since then. Mick and the Stones have soldiered on, sometimes affectingly, oftentimes not. Books have been written about them, and some of them have written books themselves (Keith Richards' memoir most notably).

Meanwhile, rock music itself has changed. Once a force, capable of challenging the dominant culture's assumptions and mores, rock has at once been subsumed into the larger entertainment industry of grazing celebrity while also being marginalized as yet another form of contemporary art—one that speaks to individuals, instead of generations. Believe it or not, the electric guitar was once a subversive instrument.

What used to be called rock has been broken into countless pieces, just like the culture that spawned it. People who hope that music might once again act as a catalyst for social or cultural change are looking in the wrong place. If there is going to be another semi-transformational moment, like the '60s, it is unlikely that music will be its engine. Some other art form or opportunity will provide the spark. These days, chefs are called "rock stars" more often than most musicians.

But this, perhaps, is also why this latest chance to see Mick and the Stones do their thing is priced on the order of a rare and vintage wine. If you want to see a rock star, this could be your last chance to experience the real thing.

Meeting a Gentleman's Gentleman
December 28, 2005

In a compulsively thumbed pocket copy of *Nicholson's Guide to London*, I find this business card. There's no logo, just a few lines of text in capital letters: CLOTHING DISCOUNT COMPANY MENSWEAR, along with an address, 6 Southampton Row in Bloomsbury. This leaves plenty of room for white space. And in that space, there is a signature in a debonair hand, "Cyril," which is underlined with a single, confident stroke.

"Hell is a city much like London," wrote the poet Shelley of this metropolis. The city is vast, crowded, and, on most days, pretty dark. It's a city where great things are promised, but anonymity is the rule. London can put a spring in your step, but it can also beat you down. Which is why every kindness that is offered there seems to count double.

My wife and I found ourselves in London at the end of October. We had been traveling for three weeks and were running low on cash, depending on plastic to carry us through the last days before our flight back to the States.

Somewhere along the way I got it in my head that I wanted to get myself a jacket as a kind of keepsake. Wherever we had gone, it seemed the men-about-town were wearing velvet blazers, the sorts of things Georgian squires might once have donned before adjourning to the library for brandy, cigars, and a grumble about the burdens of

Empire. Such a jacket, I thought to myself, would suit me to a 'T.'

I found exactly what I thought I was looking for hanging on the wall in Harrods department store. It was the color of a beaver pelt and soft as a hound's ear. Then I looked at the price tag. Based on the conversion rate of pounds to dollars, I figured the cost of this garment to be slightly less than $1,000. While I might be willing to pay that for, say, a bulletproof vest, this amount for a velvet jacket seemed decadent, even for yours truly.

In this case, though, as in so many others, self-indulgence would be the mother of invention. I remembered a corner shop near our hotel in Bloomsbury that we passed going to and from the Holborn Underground. It was an unassuming dive, rather dark and a little worn around the edges. Its display windows were crammed with menswear. It was like the place had been hit by a haberdasher's storm.

I saw the jackets almost immediately. They were a mere fraction of the price I'd come to expect. And then I met Cyril. Cyril was tall with a shock of grey hair. He wore a pressed white shirt, silk tie, and tailored trousers. He was every inch the gentleman's gentleman, what some of us today might call "old school." In another minute he was looking over my shoulder, advising (not telling) me about the proper fit.

We exchanged a few stock pleasantries. I handed Cyril my credit card to seal the deal. He ran it through his machine. "Oh dear," he said without a trace of sarcasm, "your card has been declined." Finding out that your credit is tapped out is never good news. But getting this word in London, with two days to go and a hotel bill looming, does wonders for low blood pressure.

Cyril suggested we go down the street to the Barclays Bank. "They're Visa," he said. "They'll get this cleared up."

But at Barclays the manager stared at us like we were from another galaxy. And when we tried calling 800 numbers in the US and the UK, we couldn't get through. We went to an Internet café and tried to inquire about our balance via email, but that was a bust. Getting this situation resolved looked as if it was going to take some time.

Cyril greeted me when I returned: "Well, is it good news or bad?" When I told him what had happened, he frowned. "That's horrible," he said. Before we knew it, he was reaching for his phone. "I travel a lot myself," he said, "and I know how terrible this can feel." With one hand, Cyril turned down the music he had playing on the radio, and with the other he began pounding the buttons on his plastic phone. "It's old," he apologized. "You have to hit it rather hard."

After several false starts, Cyril's eyes flashed and he handed me the phone. He had reached our credit card company in New York City. The card had been declined due to an abnormal spending pattern; we don't often eat out in Amsterdam and Brussels, and I've never tried to buy a velvet jacket. "Call us next time you're going on a trip like that," the voice in NYC told me.

I tried to pay Cyril for the cost of that call. He wouldn't hear of it. He seemed more keen on recommending a show of Degas and his contemporaries at the Tate. "If you ask me," he murmured, "that's painting."

I told Cyril that if he ever traveled to Indianapolis, dinner was on me. But odds are you, dear reader, will visit London before Cyril comes this way. If London Pride is what you're looking for, stop by 6 Southampton Row.

The Slender Thread
October 23, 2002

My son's voter registration card came in the mail yesterday. He's just turned eighteen, and he's eager to cast his first ballot on November 5. Both his parents and grandparents have encouraged him in this; for years my mother was a leader of the League of Women Voters in Chicago, so I suppose you could say our family puts a pretty high premium on showing up on Election Day.

Unfortunately, my son's eagerness to play his part in what my junior high civics teacher called "the pageant of democracy" is tempered by the fact that, with the possible exception of Julia Carson, whose vote against President Bush's war powers resolution was as courageous as it was principled, most of the candidates he'll be choosing among are hard to distinguish from one another. As both parties tailor their platforms to conform to whatever the latest polling data tells them, campaigns become more like beauty pageants than what my civics teacher had in mind.

But that's not the worst of it. Even more demoralizing for voters is the gathering suspicion that our votes aren't so much about choice as permission. That is, a vote for candidate X means that candidate is then free to go off and do whatever seems politically expedient, regardless of what his or her constituents say. For example, it was recently reported in the *Star* that although both of Indiana's senators voted to give unprecedented war powers to President Bush, Senator Lugar's mail ran 10–1 against and Senator Bayh's was 15–1 against. Did this outpouring of opposition matter? Well, senators apparently know what's best.

These votes, we were told, represented leadership, even if they didn't represent us.

Under these circumstances, it's easy to see the right to vote as being like an unlimited hall pass in a one-room schoolhouse. Is it any wonder that, when Election Day rolls around, so many of us blow it off?

This being an off-year election, without the added glamour of a presidential or even gubernatorial race to motivate voters, political observers rightly fear low voter turnout. From now through the elections, we can expect to hear a lot of earnest hand-wringing about public apathy and downright laziness, accompanied by the usual bow-wowing about how voting should be made easier, like on weekends, or via the Internet.

Such civic-mindedness seems more beside the point with each

election cycle. While there's no underestimating people's capacity for cluelessness, the fact that so many of us ignore elections as consistently as we do suggests there really is a third party in this country. Call it NONE OF THE ABOVE.

Since NOA isn't represented by anyone, there's no telling what it stands for. Indeed, the rest of us might be sorry were it to manifest itself in any practical way. Having said that, we also have to recognize the possibility that more people might vote if they had more to vote for.

The real issue isn't voter apathy, but voter disillusion. Low turnout is bred by races whose significance only pundits care about.

Which is handy for pundits and politicians alike. If our politics seems futile, it has also become more profitable for those who practice it as a kind of trade. Fewer people may be voting, but politicians rake in more cash in campaign contributions than ever.

Meanwhile, mass media journalists are paid like the entertainment stars they have actually become. What these folks have discovered is that while encouraging people to vote is good symbolism, it really doesn't matter. In fact, it might even be better if we stay at home and make politics another spectator sport. And as with every other professional sport, this means more money and less accountability for franchise players, like Sens. Bayh and Lugar.

As we learned following the last presidential go-round in 2000, TV and politics are in bed in a way that makes us—the voters—almost incidental. In the end, the Supreme Court selected the president. Meanwhile, the Florida imbroglio provided television producers with an ongoing spectacle.

Just as President Bush has equated patriotism with shopping, all of us, those who vote and those who don't, are encouraged to equate citizenship with watching. Before long, we'll stop worrying about how many of us go to the polls. Ratings—how many are tuning in for coverage — will be the number that counts.

I don't know how my son will vote or what, in the end, he will make of the experience. Voting may be an unsatisfying exercise, but it remains the slender thread that keeps us in the political picture. That so many in power would probably prefer for us to stay home only makes it more important.

A final note. Just weeks before he received his voter registration card, my son's draft card arrived in the mail. He had to request his right to vote. The draft registration came unsolicited.

A *Mad Men* Moment:
Freedom and Excess
April 18, 2012

There's a scene from an early season of the television series *Mad Men* that haunts me. *Mad Men*, as you doubtless know, is about the lives and lusts of a group of people working in a Madison Avenue advertising agency during the early 1960s. The narrative revolves around a creative director named Don Draper, a man whose identity is based on a lie: he is, quite literally, not who he says he is.

Draper's unwillingness to come to grips with his background makes for a fraught family life with his wife, Betty, and their two young children. So it comes as a relief when, in one episode, we are presented with an idyllic picture of the Draper nuclear unit enjoying a picnic lunch on the slope of a grassy hill.

We see the family from middle distance. They are finishing their meal; everyone appears smiling and carefree. This, you sense, is the kind of life moment the Drapers have always imagined for themselves. It's like one of the TV commercials from the era, in which lovers share a slow-motion embrace in a meadow full of flowers.

What haunts me about the scene is the way it ends. As the Drapers pack their picnic things, they blithely fling away their trash. Bits and scraps of newspapers used for wrapping sandwiches blow across the grass. Then they climb into Don's Cadillac and drive away.

This scene, of course, is a perfect metaphor, not just for the quality of the Draper's lives, but their American era. After living through a Great Depression and a World War, the country was booming. Americans had more of everything than anyone else in the world. We had a feast of houses and food and cars and endless amounts of entertainment. We had so much, in fact, that we could waste it, could live as if someone else would pick up after us. If this wasn't freedom, what was?

The underlying theme of *Mad Men*—and the reason this series is about a lot more than the groggy joys of lunchtime martinis, office trysts, and smoking three packs a day—is about what happens when people confuse freedom with excess. Freedom is a word that's easily said, but hard to actually understand. It's an abstraction that can mean different things to different people. Freedom means one thing if you live in a country that outlaws blue jeans and rock and roll. It likely means something else to a person with unlimited Internet access and a Nordstrom's charge account.

But anybody can understand the freedom to throw their trash out a window, smoke or drink whenever and wherever they damn well please, or dump whatever bores them, be it a meal, an outfit, or an unruly pet.

It was in the '60s that rock bands began making a sport of trashing hotel rooms. Some bands were notorious for the lengths they'd go to in systematically ruining the spaces they rented for a night or two. Was it because the room service was bad or the mattresses too lumpy? No, bands did it because they could. Their managers paid for the damages. This was freedom.

America calls itself the land of the free. Lacking a definition for what this might actually mean—or the discipline to come up with one—we have, like the characters in *Mad Men*, hit the default button in favor of excess. Through various forms of government subsidy we have willfully manipulated our supposedly "free" marketplace to artificially suppress the prices we pay for fuel and food. We wonder why our air isn't better or how so many of us got to be obese. But heaven help the fool with the impertinence to suggest that maybe, just maybe, we might be better off if the prices we paid for things reflected what they actually cost.

The same thing applies to one of our most cherished freedoms, the freedom of speech. People pride themselves on being "free speech absolutists," thereby lending cover to commercial interests that use this freedom to send heaping doses of graphically portrayed sexual violence into people's homes via an increasing array of media at all hours. Whatever the consequences of this stuff may be, its purveyors say it's not their problem. You see, the rest of us are free to steer clear of what they do—if, that is, we can.

The poet William Blake once wrote words to the effect that we never know what's enough until we experience too much. That is probably true. But the problem with defining freedom in terms of our excesses is that it substitutes imaginative impoverishment for genuine abundance. It doesn't take imagination to keep doing the same thing again and again until exhaustion sets in. On the other hand, a creative leap is required to envision all that might be possible should we set about trying something really new.

In *Mad Men*, Don Draper, quintessential imperial American male, goes to extraordinary lengths to maintain his false front. This front, he thinks, has liberated him from a suffocating past. We can see, though, that he's running himself into the ground. Whether he has the capacity to change—whether, that is, Don can ever truly be free—remains to be seen.

The House on Memory Lane:
A Look Back
June 8, 2011

I grew up in Mt. Prospect, Illinois, a suburb northwest of Chicago. When I was a kid, it seemed the city was a long way off, another world. But when I went back for a visit recently, it only took us about thirty minutes to drive from my son's apartment on Chicago's north side to my old front door on, I kid you not, a street called Memory Lane.

My wife and son had never seen the place where I was raised. I'm not sure why we put the trip off for such a long time; we've often visited Chicago over the years, and my son even went to college there. It would have been easy.

But other things grabbed our attention, and, besides, when it came right down to it, I couldn't think of anything we could actually do in Mt. Prospect.

I remember a conversation I had with a good high school buddy, Paul Lembesis, one night when we were about to graduate. The two of us were walking the typically quiet streets around my neighborhood, and Paul observed that Mt. Prospect had been a great place to grow up, but there really wasn't anything about it to hold us there.

A lot of time has passed since then. My son not only graduated from high school, he graduated from college. Meanwhile, my parents, the people who brought me up in that house on Memory Lane, have moved on. They sold the place almost forty years ago. Now they're looking after each other, valiantly contending with the unforgiving indignities that, all too often, attend the end of life in America.

I suspect my parents are the reason why I finally wanted to make the trip to Mt. Prospect. I wanted to think of them the way they were in those days. And I wanted my family to understand something about them that maybe couldn't be grasped in any other way.

When my parents bought that house in 1950, there was a cornfield at the end of the street. The realtor who sold them the place gestured toward the sun as it set over those rows of corn and said, "It'll be like this forever!" That, of course, was bunk. By the time I was ten, the cornfield had been turned into athletic fields for the high school Paul and I and thousands like us would attend.

It was the Baby Boom. The guys who served in World War II had come home, gotten married, and started families. They moved to places like Mt. Prospect, turning it from a small farming town along a set of railway tracks into a Chicago bedroom community, a place dedicated to raising kids.

Raising kids is what I think of when I hear people talk about "the Greatest Generation." As important as their service was in wartime, that generation's commitment to their kids' quality of life may have been even greater.

In many ways it was a massive improvisation. Nothing like it had ever been tried. Not only did these new veterans create communities for kids, they equipped these places with state-of-the-art schools, YMCAs, public swimming pools, ice rinks, Girl and Boy Scout troops, Little Leagues, and more. Some even say the very idea of being a "teenager" took hold at this time, as did the expectation that everyone should go to college, nurtured by our parents' unprecedented postwar experience of higher education thanks to the tax-supported G.I. Bill.

If this sounds like a kind of utopia, it wasn't. Although my dad made a point of regularly playing catch with me after driving back from his job in the city, too many fathers were absent for large chunks of time. Too many moms suffered from undiagnosed depression. And the rage to conform—think of Benjamin Braddock in *The Graduate*—could be soul destroying.

Still, as I drove by the blocks of tidy single family homes in Mt. Prospect, it was hard not to feel that for all its flaws, this place had succeeded in making something that's too rare in America: a culture. Although part of Cook County, Mt. Prospect was a politically conservative place when I was growing up. Barry Goldwater carried it with ease while being trounced almost everywhere else during the 1964 presidential election.

Yet this conservatism didn't keep the people there from building and sustaining an outstanding public school system. Yes, homeowners were expected to be responsible for themselves. The mostly modest-size houses still appear to be feverishly tended. But the quality of the schools made a shared sense of aspiration palpable. Kids really did come before politics, and, while I am somewhat sorry to say it, this is probably because we pretty much looked the same and came from similarly striving homes.

What strikes me now is how such an extraordinary accomplishment could, on the surface, appear so ordinary—and how easily it could be taken for granted. I was lucky to have grown up where I did. Although I'll never live there again, I'm glad to be reminded that it's closer than I thought.

Personal Indianapolis

My family and I moved to Indianapolis in 1988. The Pacers played at Market Square Arena and the Colts at the Hoosier Dome. Circle Centre Mall was a vast hole in the ground. As the years went by, if someone asked me how I thought things were going, I often said they seemed to be getting a little more complicated—a good thing, as far as I'm concerned. The heroes here tend to be local, like the Good Earth's dear departed Bob Landman, the Jazz Kitchen's Dave Allee, and, for my money, the city's poet laureate, Mari Evans. Oh, and how about those Butler Bulldogs?

Backyard Stars
June 21, 2006

The other night, as my dog and I were making our usual circuit around the neighborhood park near our house, I looked up at the sky and saw stars. This is not an unusual occurrence. When it's clear, a few stars are usually visible overhead. I'm not a student of these things, but on the best nights even I can identify a constellation or two. And when this happens, as it did the other night, I am reminded, again, why I'm glad to be living in this town.

I'm not immune to fantasizing about what it would be like to live in other places. Like most people I know, I seem to spend a fair amount of time weighing the pros and cons of different destinations. In my experience, that's Indianapolis' favorite form of table talk. Whereas in New York people are forever talking and conniving about the availability of a better apartment, and in Chicago they obsess about hot, new neighborhoods, in Indianapolis we talk about whether or not to pull up stakes altogether for some other, presumably better, city.

Make no mistake, there are plenty of things around here that seem custom-tailored to get a person's goat. If chamber-of-commerce-style cheerleading were an art form, Indianapolis would build a museum to honor it—and try to do it on the cheap.

I find that I'm often thinking about this kind of craziness as I'm fumbling with my dog's leash or pulling on my shoes in preparation for our evening constitutional. Then we step outside.

Sometimes what we find out there is almost disconcerting. Depending on the weather, people might be partying, there's live music playing in the middle distance, and, on occasion, the sky will be raked by celebratory searchlights. My dog and I know that if we walk in a certain direction for another ten minutes, we'll be in the thick of it.

Most nights, though, it feels as if we're five miles from nowhere in particular. The streetlight at the end of the block casts a pale light across the peak of an old, wood-frame garage, and, if you didn't know better, you'd think this was the edge of farm country. It's that quiet.

Indianapolis has a split personality, there's no doubt about it. For every one of us who can't wait for this place to grow up and be truly urban, there's someone else who says, "Hold on, not so fast." This ambivalence can cause problems. It manifests itself, among other things, in suburban sprawl, undistinguished downtown architecture, and an unwillingness to come to grips with what it costs to make a big city work. We keep hoping we can be the biggest little town in America when it's plain that's like a forty-year-old man trying to fit into his high-school jeans.

But this is not an either/or problem. Personally, I like the way this town, at its best, blends urbanity and nature. Take a canoe ride down the White River some time. You'll find yourself amazed at how quickly you can go from seeing a blue heron to having dinner on Massachusetts Avenue.

Many cities are defined by their downtown architecture. We've shortchanged ourselves in this department, it's true. But it is just as true that you can't get Indianapolis until you venture into our neighborhoods. The key to this city lies in the quality and variety of its residential architecture. This is ultimately a city of homes, of backyards and gardens. I'm not talking here about the decorator porn you see in *Indianapolis Monthly*. We're more abundant, more bumptious, and more fun than that.

On Memorial Day weekend I stood in the backyard of one of my neighbors, cracking open freshly boiled crawfish with about fifty other lucky folks. The crawfish were spicy and the beer was cold. Parents and kids licked their fingers and stood chatting or wandered off. I counted three, maybe four generations there. People who hardly knew one another talked about the race and the exploits of racecar drivers in an easy, half-joking way. It was a beautiful Indianapolis afternoon.

Last week I saw an item on the evening news about the high cost of new downtown condos. Apparently people are paying as much as a million bucks to live in the heart of our fair city. Insofar as this makes Indianapolis appear to be in a league with other big cities, this, I guess, is good news.

But I will continue to think that Indy's ultimate success will be based less on trying to be like other cities than on identifying those local characteristics that set us apart. What, in other words, should it mean to live in this medium-size midwestern place now that we're in the twenty-first century?

I'm not sure yet how to answer that question. But I know this: in most cities of any size, the lights are so bright they make it impossible to see the stars at night. You have to drive out beyond the city limits if you want to look at the Big Dipper or Orion's Belt. In Indianapolis, if it's not too cloudy, I can see them every night when my dog and I go walking.

Bob Landman's Business Model: The Good Earth
December 17, 2008

It's fascinating how some people and places can become a valuable part of you without even seeming to try. Now that he's gone, I realize that Bob Landman was like that for me. Bob was proprietor of the Good Earth Natural Food Store in Broad Ripple. He passed away on December 6, a Saturday night, at the age of sixty-two.

I can walk to the Good Earth from where I live. I've shopped there for twenty years. Despite that, I can't say I really knew Bob. He read this column from time to time and was generous enough to say so if we bumped into each other in one of his store's narrow passageways. But, mainly, he was a friendly, helpful presence. Whenever I saw Bob, it seemed he was helping someone find a pair of shoes that fit, or the right vitamin supplement, or the freshest, greatest tasting apple.

Much, quite rightly, has been made of Bob's prescience in getting in on the ground floor of the healthy foods business in the early 1970s. Those were the days when "health food store" had a countercultural ring to it. Rather than futuristic, these emporiums usually had a handmade, frontier feel about them. This reflected the larger ethos of the counterculture that, contrary to the let-it-all-hang-out stereotypes propounded by mainstream media, was actually conservative in the truest sense. Conservative, that is, in wanting to keep alive such supposedly traditional American values as fair dealing, respect for authenticity, and the preservation of local cultural identity.

These are the values, of course, most endangered in a country where a premium is placed on being big, where it's said you must grow or die, and where success is defined as market domination. And so, as the Good Earth went from being the only store of its kind around here to little guy in a sea of heavily capitalized franchises from other parts of the country, those of us who patronized the place found ourselves flinching a little. We worried that Wild Oats would be too big, or that Sunflower would be too close. We saw neighborhood hardware stores and drugstores disappearing, and we feared the Good Earth might be overtaken as well.

But the Good Earth has survived because Bob Landman and the team of individuals who make up the Good Earth family stuck to their core principles. Yes, it's true that Landman and crew were on to the next big thing when they hitched their wagon to organic products and local foods—what in business parlance could be called an emerging trend. But if that was all they had going for them, the Good Earth would have been swamped by the competition long ago.

"Our marketing strategy has always been to just offer the best possible prices on everything all the time," Landman told the *Indianapolis Business Journal* in 1999, trying his best to speak in terms the readers of that publication might understand. I'd like to think there was a larger message embedded in that statement, something about what I think Bob understood regarding the relationship any business needs to have with the community where it lives.

A community isn't just a market to be exploited. It's a web of relationships. A problem for business is that as it gets bigger, it also finds nourishing certain kinds of community relationships more difficult. It becomes more impersonal. At this point, such businesses try various marketing ploys to make it seem like they "care." Meanwhile, their rage for growth continues.

The Good Earth is not a service organization. Bob Landman needed to make a profit. But his idea of growth seemed founded not on the sheer number, but the quality of the relationships he could cultivate. And so the Good Earth held its ground, made adjustments as required, but never wavered from its (counter) cultural principles.

I wonder if Bob paid attention to economic theory in the Himalayan kingdom of Bhutan. In that country, they don't measure the Gross Domestic Product. Instead, since 1972, they have developed a way to gauge their prosperity based on what they call Gross National Happiness (GNH). For GNH to grow, the Bhutanese focus on four key areas: the promotion of equitable and sustainable socioeconomic development; preservation and promotion of cultural values; conservation of the environment; and good government. "Happiness is very serious business," according to Bhutan's prime minister, Jigme Thinley. "The dogma of limitless productivity and growth in a finite world is unsustainable and unfair for future generations."

With the possible exception of that serious part, I suspect Bob Landman would have known exactly what the prime minister is talking about. Sustainable happiness was at the heart of Bob's business model.

Sorry, This Is Not a Great
Sports Town: Indy's Creation Myth
March 18, 2009

Every place has an origin story, a folk tale that's handed down from one generation to the next about how things got started. Indianapolis is no exception. The Indianapolis story goes something like this: once upon a time, back in the 1970s, a bunch of rising young Indianapolis business executives discovered they had one thing in common—they were all unhappy with living in a town other people called "India-no-place."

When these young executives looked in the mirror each morning and straightened their ties, they saw a bunch of smart, ambitious guys staring back. These were not the faces of men who made their living in a town where it was said the sidewalks were rolled up each night at 5 p.m. No!

The young executives met regularly to drown their sorrows and brainstorm about what it would take to transform their town. They agreed what was needed was a hook: a governing image or theme. Something easy for their fellow townsfolk to understand and rally around.

No one knows for sure who had the idea first. Heck, even if they did know they'd be too modest to admit it. What matters is that one day those young executives looked into one another's eyes with the certain knowledge that they'd got it: Indianapolis would be Amateur Sports Capital of the World.

When the city succeeded in attracting the Pan Am Games in 1987, it looked as if this strategy had paid off. Not only was Indy about to host a significant international event, the sports theme helped to reinvigorate downtown investment and construction. Those young business executives drifted into middle age, content with the knowledge that Indianapolis wasn't no-place any more.

But a couple of things happened on our way to becoming a sports capital. The first was that we let the success of what amounted to a marketing strategy persuade us Indianapolis was actually a great sports town, full of people with an insatiable appetite for games.

We also (very quietly) dropped the amateur part of the equation. But we don't care more about sports than people do anywhere else. What we really like is spectacle. The Pan Am Games was a spectacle. Apart from the occasional Final Four tournament, most amateur athletics never rise to that level. So, while being an amateur sports capital might be fun for the athletes, their families, and the media involved, it's not generally a huge deal for the city. People come here for Olympic-class track and swimming trials, for example, and hardly anyone notices.

The other thing that people in Indy, like people everywhere, go for is celebrity. With the exception of a rare bird like Michael Phelps, few amateur athletes qualify. For this, you need professional sports. With its pro men's and women's basketball and football franchises, annual tennis tournament, periodic professional golf events, and, of course, motor racing, Indianapolis has arguably invested more in the pros than it ever did in amateur athletics.

This has been great for local media hacks, who understandably love their big-time beats. They have tirelessly promoted the idea of Indy as a great sports town and the sports capital strategy as a brilliant stroke. There's more self-serving enthusiasm than substance in these claims.

Exhibit A is the Pacers. Hoosiers supposedly can't get enough basketball. But the Pacers are one of the most poorly attended teams in the NBA. Local media keeps saying this is because of a spell of player thuggishness. But if that spell had coincided with a team capable of playing deep into the playoffs, fans would doubtless have embraced the villains as lovable rascals.

The same holds true for the Colts. Before the Peyton Manning era, good seats in the Dome were always available. When Manning finally hangs it up, we'll see what happens. Local sports pundits like to say the Super Bowl champs have turned Indy into a "football town." No, like any town, Indy likes a winner.

Last week, Pacers owner Herb Simon told the *Indianapolis Star* his family can't afford to keep the Pacers going without some form of financial help. The team, in this supposedly great sports town, has reportedly lost $200 million since 1983. They want someone—probably you and me—to pick up the $15 million annual tab for their use of Conseco Fieldhouse.

This is when people start saying things like, "To be a major league city, you have to have major league teams." The truth is, to be major league you have to have a bunch of major corporate headquarters in your city. Neither the Pacers' trip to the NBA Finals in 2000 nor the Colts Super Bowl win in 2006 netted us so much as one Fortune 500 company.

Dear CIB: You want to be major league? Try fixing the streets, the schools, and public safety. Make Indianapolis known as the best-run town of its size in America. I'm sure the old guys who dreamt up the sports strategy way back when would have no objections. All they wanted was an idea that worked.

Friday Night at the Jazz Kitchen: Tasting Tradition
July 2, 2008

The other night I found myself in one of my favorite places, Dave Allee's Jazz Kitchen. If, when I was a teenager, you'd asked me to describe the ideal nightclub, there's a good chance I would have come up with a fair approximation of what Dave has going at the corner of Fifty-Fourth and College. The room has warm light and great shadows. People look good there. The food is delicious. The cocktails are sincere. And the jazz...the jazz is great.

On the night in question, Dave's dad, the pianist and jazz composer Steve Allee, was celebrating the release of a new album with rhythm masters Frank Smith and Kenny Phelps on bass and drums and saxophonist Rob Dixon. They swung through a set of new tunes with joyful intensity, confirming the home truth that jazz is best experienced live.

Tradition is a word that gets tossed around a lot when it comes to jazz, especially in Indianapolis. It's meant to signify the fact that the family tree of this most American of arts has a special branch with our city's name on it. Jazz history has been made here and exported to the larger world by such names as Hampton, Johnson, Montgomery, and Hubbard. Scholars can write books about it.

But it takes more than history to make a tradition. That's because tradition is a living thing that needs to keep its body limber. Otherwise, it gets stiff and calcified, and, before you know it, the only place you're liable to find it is under glass in a museum.

Tradition is not past tense. It is all about the present, but with that something extra that comes of knowing that what's happening now is informed and inspired by stories, lives, and works that came before. To be in the presence of a living tradition is not to be made to think about the past, necessarily, so much as to be able to taste it. The flavor is rich.

That's what I get at the Jazz Kitchen. It's what Messrs Allee, Smith, Phelps, and Dixon were providing on the bandstand. It reminded me that, at a time when there's no end of speculation about what might happen to the music business, the art of making music is as vital as ever, buttressed by a great heritage that's being reinvented wherever committed musicians gather.

This is not to say that all's well for the arts economy. As the critic Walter Benjamin so famously put it, the big story for the arts in the twentieth century had to do with their "mechanical reproduction." The invention, that is, of ways of turning one-of-a-kind experiences into mass-produced items. Once, if you wanted to hear music, you either had to make it yourself, or go someplace where other people were performing. Recordings changed that. They made it possible for us to listen to what we wanted, when we wanted, without leaving the house. The same thing was true of reproductions of famous paintings, the broadcast of performing arts on TV and, more recently, the recording and distribution of movies.

Mechanical reproduction gave birth to a business model that made a lot of money for a lot of people. It still works to some degree, but the Internet has made it clear that the twentieth-century business model is all but finished. What takes its place is hard to say. In a world where anyone can record an album and everyone can download it for free—well, let's just say mechanical reproduction ain't what it used to be.

Which brings me back to the Jazz Kitchen, to four seasoned players communicating with one another on the fly, making something in the moment that wasn't there a moment before. A rich tradition brought to life. The trouble, though, is that the twentieth century wasn't that long ago. For many of us, myself included, the analog habits of the couch, the CD player, and the television set—the trinity of home entertainment—remain potent.

But they are also becoming less persuasive. As album sales dwindle, musicians of all sorts are increasingly rediscovering the importance of what can't be duplicated, building careers on the foundation of live performance. What goes around, comes around. And, for my money, one of the best places to catch it is at the corner of Fifty-Fourth and College.

Poetry Meets Power:
Black Arts Movement Reunion
May 2, 2012

A couple of weeks ago, the Etheridge Knight Festival of the Arts presented Indianapolis with an extraordinary gift. Now in its twenty-first incarnation, the festival, created by Eunice Knight-Bowens, is named in honor of her brother and one of this city's most renowned poets.

Etheridge Knight lived a hard life, doing time in prison and struggling with drug and alcohol addiction. But he was also possessed of an eloquent, resonant voice, which managed to reach an enormous audience. When he died in 1991, poets from across the country came to Indianapolis for a reading in his honor at the Athenaeum.

Those of us who were lucky enough to be at the Athenaeum that night witnessed what amounted to one of the exclamation points in Indianapolis' cultural history. Something similar took place April 19, in the splendidly refurbished hall of the Indiana Landmarks Center, formerly known as the Old Centrum.

"An Evening With the Legends" was a gathering of four poets, Amiri Baraka, Mari Evans, Haki Madhubuti, and Sonia Sanchez—all of whom were either founding or pivotal members of the Black Arts Movement that coalesced in the wake of the assassination of Malcolm X during the mid-1960s.

To get a sense of the significance of this event, imagine finding such prototypical Beat poets as Allen Ginsberg, Gary Snyder, Lawrence Ferlinghetti, and Michael McClure on the same stage. Or, for that matter, a collection of modernist masters like Ezra Pound, William Carlos Williams, Wallace Stevens, and T. S. Eliot.

Let's just say the iconic quotient in the room on April 19 was formidable. The place was packed. In part, I suspect this was thanks to the participation of local poet, essayist, and activist Mari Evans. If Indianapolis were to adopt the appellation of Living Treasure, as they do in Japan, to recognize the true masters among us, Ms. Evans would surely be first in line. The audience leapt to its feet when she made her way to the stage.

But something else was going on. This was not just any gathering of literary stars. The Black Arts Movement represented a particular and provocative approach to art and society. It still does. As Kaluma ya Salaam has written, "Both inherently and overtly political in content, the Black Arts movement was the only American literary movement to advance 'social engagement' as a sine qua non of its aesthetic. The movement broke from the immediate past of protest and petition (civil rights) literature and dashed forward toward an alternative that initially seemed unthinkable and unobtainable: Black Power."

Since the first election of Ronald Reagan, the arts in America have been under virtual siege. Conservative politicians have, to a large extent, succeeded in caricaturing the arts as pointy-headed, liberal, elitist, and commercially out of touch with mass appetites.

Arts advocates have tried to defend themselves against these attacks by arguing for the arts' democratization, emphasizing inclusive outreach programs and cultural diversity—the idea that the arts are the one place in America's multicultural gumbo where we can all hold hands and get along.

The legacy of the Black Arts Movement suggests we tack in a radically different direction. By unabashedly asserting that they were black, other, and systematically oppressed, these artists didn't just challenge the validity so many Americans traditionally placed on the idea of cultural assimilation or the melting pot. Their insistent focus on the nature of power relations in our society—making power's many guises an unavoidable subject in the poetic landscape—also unmasked attacks on the arts as attempts on behalf of the status quo to reduce forms of expression to entertainment aimed at keeping us fat, pleased with ourselves, and dumb.

If you read the history, it is tempting to think the Black Arts Movement was volatile but brief, its social impact negligible. As Mari Evans pointed out in her remarks, black males today are in serious trouble; one out of three black males born today is expected to go to prison. Sonia Sanchez warned that, at this rate, a truly African American population might be extinct in this country come the twenty-second century. But then, the country also has its first black president, a fact that doesn't validate Black Power so much as give it a tragic spin.

Art that makes social change part of its aesthetic takes a big risk. It dares to be judged not just in terms of how it affects what goes on in people's heads, but by what goes on in the world. This is usually a losing proposition. That's why when artists who have been through a fiery time together reunite, they often do little more than recall the way things were. But the artists who assembled on April 19 were not looking back. Their performances were driven by unabated urgency. Their language was often charged with the ring of prophecy. They were black, yes, but the power they spoke of, the ways it is abused and how that defines us, is ultimately colorblind.

Human Scale:
So Long to the Big City
September 21, 2011

I was visiting my neighborhood bank the other day, doing a little of what I, in my more tripped-out moments, like to call "business." While in the midst of this transaction, a fellow sauntered in and went to the window beside mine, where he and the teller exchanged a pleasant greeting.

The teller asked the new arrival how his weekend went. "Exciting," he replied. "I was up in Chicago. Had a great time. Glad I don't live there, though."

As someone who grew up in what our neighbors to the north so fancifully call "Chicagoland," I couldn't help but be intrigued by what this guy said. It actually made a lot of sense to me.

My son recently moved away from Chicago. He'd lived there for the past eight years, first as a college student and then, after graduation, in the kind of indentured servitude that is the lot of so many people in their twenties who graduate with a bachelor's degree in the liberal arts.

My son loved Chicago in many ways. His grandparents and great grandparents were Chicagoans; he was introduced to the city at an early age and grew up aspiring to make its brawny scale and accelerated rhythms his own.

His mother and I encouraged him in this. Like the members of so many generations before us, we thought Chicago's size and scope represented a wealth of opportunity, especially for a bright kid who was starting out in life.

That's not the way things played out.

The great Chicago novelist Nelson Algren famously called Chicago a "city on the make." He was referring to the appetite the mid-twentieth-century metropolis he knew so well had for making money, making deals, making things happen. Whether these deals were made on the table or under it didn't matter so long as you got yours, and there was plenty to go around. Mayor Richard Daley the First—father of the recently retired Ritchie the Second—was known as The Boss in those days; he had signs put up that proclaimed Chicago to be "the city that works."

After applying to over two hundred places, my son wasn't so sure about that. Oh, he wound up getting a job—with low pay, long hours, and zero benefits—the standard issue for college grads without a technical degree or a taste for high finance. He was glad to have it! And he stuck with it for two years, working some days from eight in the morning until eleven at night, because he knew if he quit, there'd be a line of people eager to take his place.

This wasn't exactly the Chicago life my son pictured for himself. Not that he minded scuffling for a living; he knew that was likely to be part of the deal. But he thought there might be some sliver of light at the end of his particular tunnel, a chance to get a leg up.

Unfortunately for him, Chicago didn't seem so much on the make as made. Its public transit system, which he used every day, was unreliable. The cost of living was always going up, and taxes were never-ending. The Chicago for people with money seemed to be getting farther and farther away from all those people who had just enough to get by.

My son moved to Greensboro, North Carolina, in July. Greensboro has a population of 270,000, compared to Chicago's three million. In Chicago there are approximately 12,750 people packed into every square mile; I doubt they even bother to count such things in Greensboro.

In Greensboro, my son and his partner live in twice the space for about half the rent they paid in Chicago. Sure, downtown Greensboro is rather pokey compared to the Mag Mile, but there are decent places to eat locally grown food, the beer is great, and there's a lively arts and music scene.

More to the point: my son found a job within a month of setting foot in the place. Still no benefits, but there seems to be opportunity for growth.

Greensboro may lack Chicago's outsized panache, but it has something Chicago seems to be losing: human scale. Chicago and other American megacities reflect the structural decay of our economy. They are increasingly designed for the benefit of that small fraction of the population who possess a disproportionate share of the wealth and whose buying power drives the cost of almost everything to the edge of most people's means. Wherever you have a city with a large financial sector, you have a city that teeters on being unaffordable.

This means that cities like Greensboro and, for that matter, Indianapolis, are the new centers for opportunity, especially for young, creative adults who aren't ready to be programmed on to a one-track career path. These are places where face-to-face interaction is still possible; where people can matter.

After a lifetime of being told that bigger is better, that growth is the measure of all things, maybe we're about to discover something new: that cities where we can actually live may be the most exciting places of all.

Dinner at Traders Point: Words Matter
July 20, 2005

Traders Point, the bucolic enclave on the city's far northwest side, feels a world away from downtown Indianapolis. But owing to its proximity to freeways, it actually takes less time to drive downtown from Traders Point than it does from Broad Ripple. This is a blessing and a curse. It makes commuting easy for people who work downtown but want to get away from it all when they return home at night. It also makes Traders Point an irresistible morsel for developers who would turn its genuine country charm into yet another level hunk of upscale suburbia.

This troublesome observation is duly noted and set aside. That's because it's Friday evening at the Traders Point Creamery. The time before sunset that photographers call "the golden hour." Light burnishes the trees and meadows. Even dust in the air looks precious.

A crowd of us is sitting on a deck eating fresh chicken salad, slaw, and soba noodles with green beans that taste like they just came out of the garden. There's lemonade, bottled water, and, of course, cold bottles of that Traders Point chocolate milk.

Finding this place was a little like coming upon a big family party. After we parked our car at the end of a gravel driveway, we strolled through a friendly gauntlet of local growers offering us fresh produce, meats, honey, and bouquets of flowers. The dishes on offer for this evening's meal were written on a chalkboard.

From where we sit we can see a pond and, at a distance, a herd of dairy cattle. When we finish eating we get up and explore. There's a barn with a basketball hoop attached to a beam inside (how Indiana is that?). We meet a trio of newborn calves. Free-range chickens are, in fact, ranging freely and, beneath the branches of a shade tree, we can see a swimming hole in which kids are actually swimming. Up in the visitor's center, a young woman makes me one of the best milkshakes I've ever had. Then we all go downstairs and load up on milk and cheese and meat to take home. We pay for everything using the honor system. On the way out, my son says, "If this place was in northern California, it would be famous." He's probably right.

This, however, is Indiana. What that means, exactly, is hard to say. I am speaking quite literally here. Studies have been done that indicate we Hoosiers have a difficult time articulating what it is that makes our place special. It's easier for us to tell other people what we don't have (mountains, seashore, celebrities) than what we do (places like Traders Point). Our inability to talk about the qualities of our place has consequences. It makes us think that something here doesn't measure up—as if the lack of words we have for something signifies a great emptiness.

Well, it's not just nature that abhors a vacuum. Ugliness can't stand it either. Our loss for words about Indiana has given people license to do their worst to a landscape that's easily exploited—especially when no one stands up for it with language as powerful as the urge to make a quick buck.

Governor Mitch Daniels provides a case in point. During his campaign Daniels crisscrossed the state, stopping in small towns and singing the virtues of the Hoosier sense of place. He emphasized stories of how individuals have worked, often against the odds, to create a distinctive quality of life for themselves and their communities.

You'd think that a place like the Traders Point Creamery would exemplify what Daniels likes best about Indiana. Here are people who are putting the culture back in agriculture. Not only are they creating great-tasting and wholesome products, they're doing it in ways that respect the land and the animals from which these products are derived. They are offering a model that connects the best practices of Indiana's farming past with a world hungry for the unadulterated and the authentic. You'd think Daniels would look at Traders Point Creamery and see the future.

Unfortunately, it's agribusiness, not agriculture, which gets Daniels' attention. Instead of making Indiana a brand synonymous with quality and care, he wants, for the sake of productivity and profit, to double the number of our industrial hog farms. If this turns large portions of rural Indiana into corporate colonies and makes the air in these places unfit to breathe—so what? It's only Indiana, a place without so much as a vocabulary to defend itself.

Farewell to another Borders: The End of an Era
April 13, 2011

I visited the Borders store up at River Crossing last week. It was a melancholy experience.

Borders filed for Chapter 11 bankruptcy reorganization in February. Since then they've announced the imminent closure of more than two hundred stores around the country. Their downtown store, at the intersection of Washington and Meridian, was on an initial list of "underperforming" franchises. The River Crossing store was added in a second round of cuts. It's expected to go dark in May.

Although the banner signs proclaiming everything on sale were designed to boost a glad-handing holiday atmosphere, there was a hush about the store when I stopped in. The shelves were still well stocked and there were plenty of people milling about, but it felt a little like everyone was laying in supplies before a storm.

Or the end of an era.

Borders stores have been with us, in one form or another, for such a long time now that it's hard to imagine Indianapolis without them. When Borders opened its first store in Castleton in the 1980s, it was a cultural event. The city really didn't have an all-purpose bookstore, and Borders, with its massive inventory, was phenomenal, a great whoop of affirmation for smart people throughout the city.

Thanks to the leadership of its local management team, headed by a literate entrepreneur named Cecelie Field, the first Borders store never felt like a chain. It was, instead, a gathering place, an oasis for people hungry for books and ideas.

It was also, it must be noted, a bookstore. There was no music. No DVDs. No coffee bar, either. What's more, though the place was commodious, it wasn't a big box. It was, instead, just big enough to feel robustly overstuffed, as if the store was a metaphor for a generous mind.

Our Borders was such a success that, when Indianapolis threw its first citywide book festival, Wordstruck, in 1991, Tom Borders, one of the two founding Borders brothers, came down from the home office in Ann Arbor for an opening night dinner with Kurt Vonnegut.

Those were the days.

Books! books! were a hot commodity. In 1992 the Borders brothers sold their business to Kmart, which proceeded to create the multimedia superstore in order to compete with Barnes and Noble, another booming book franchise coming out of New York. Now, in addition to row upon row of books, you could also choose among thousands of CDs, and on and on.

Borders and Barnes and Noble became known for predatory business practices. If they found a neighborhood with a successful independent bookseller, they would build a superstore across the street or down the block. Readers, being addicts of a sort, couldn't resist. Whatever loyalty they felt toward their independent suppliers was trumped by the chains' abundant inventory. The independent bookstore, a previously indispensable part of any cultural scene worth its salt, became an endangered species.

Meanwhile, Indianapolis went from having one Borders to several.

It seemed the corporate honchos at Kmart never saw Amazon coming. But that's what happened. Suddenly anybody with a computer had every book in print (and many that weren't) just a few keystrokes away.

And now, with e-readers, books themselves are becoming a thing of the past.

This, of course, is evolution, the river of commerce rolling by. Things change. But as I meandered through the tall stacks at Borders' River Crossing store, I was reminded of what a serendipitous pleasure bookstore browsing, in three dimensions, in real time, can be. I wasn't looking for a particular book or even a subject area. I had no goal in mind. So I started in fiction, thumbing through Mark Twain and Martin Amis. Then to gardening, where I spied a book about growing plants in shady places. In another section I stumbled upon Cornelius Ryan's *The Longest Day*, a classic account of the Normandy invasion that taught my eighth-grade self some things about storytelling that I still carry to this day.

I found books by authors I'd never heard of before. Read blurbs on back covers. And came upon this oddly disconcerting admission in a collection of essays by Montaigne: "I do not know whether I would much rather have produced a perfectly formed child by intercourse with the Muses than by intercourse with my wife."

As I wandered among the books, I wondered how anyone might ever again be tempted to pick up something they knew nothing about by an author they'd never heard of. Amazon, I know, will helpfully tell you that if you like this, you might like that. But that's like asking for directions. It substitutes intention for intuition and can't compare to the discoveries you make yourself.

The good news in all this is that, for the moment at least, smaller, independent bookstores appear to be making a modest comeback.

What they lack in inventory they make up for in community. Like great cafes, they serve as gathering places where people meet to share enthusiasms—which, with all due respect to Montaigne, have always seemed better served in the flesh.

Walking the Dog: Finding My Neighborhood
July 12, 2005

I met my neighbor Barb in the park the other day. I hadn't seen her in ages—months, probably. "You need to get a dog," she told me.

My dog, George, died in March over a year ago. His passing was a blow to everyone in our family. He'd seen our son grow up from a kindergartner to a college student. At night, while my wife and I were dreaming, his snoring was the background music. His barking kept our house safe from all forms of villainy.

Most of all, George took me for walks.

George was a cross between a collie and a golden lab, working breeds that need plenty of exercise. It took three walks a day to keep him healthy and in good spirits. Luckily for us, we lived near a small park. First thing in the morning and late at night, George and I would make a tour of this place. It was George's job to make sure that all the trees were still there and to conduct an inventory of its myriad smells. As for me, these jaunts were an invaluable way of keeping in touch with my neighborhood.

Whether I was finding gang signs spray painted in the alley, or a posting on the tennis courts proclaiming the start of another season of junior lessons, when I was walking the dog I felt like I had a better sense of what was going on. One summer, a lone guy used to park his car by the park every night just after nine o'clock. Needless to say, George and I kept an eye on him. Another year, some guy who'd probably been thrown out of his place slept there in his van. And then there was the period when, every morning, George and I would catch sight of a haunted-looking young woman across the park who seemed to be training for a sport that no one but her would probably ever understand. If she thought we were watching, she'd disappear around a corner.

One night as George and I walked down the alley on the far side of the park, I spied a couple of guys skulking in a yard behind someone's house. This was an unusual enough occurrence that I called the police when I got home. "Wow," said the dispatcher when I told her I'd been walking in the alley after 11:30. "Do you think that's safe?" Sure, I said, I was with my dog.

Going out with George was a spontaneous blend of the solitary and the social. Although it wasn't unusual for us to make it around the park without seeing so much as the odd feral cat or bumblebee, our walks were always enhanced by encounters with fellow dogs—and dog walkers.

There was Barb, of course, with her black and white-freckled pooch. We'd stop, and while the dogs flirted and then became bored, the two of us talked—politics (usually pissed off), books (usually enthused), kids and grandkids (ecstatic). When the weather was bad, the ground covered with ice or the wind whipping rain, we gestured to one another, showing solidarity in misery.

Mornings I got used to finding Joe walking with his pug, Buddy. Joe was a retired gent and Buddy his companion. Though Buddy stood about knee-high to George, he seemed to want to hang with the big dog. George was cool with it. There was the obligatory butt sniff followed by a tolerant condescension. Joe and I talked about our dogs, the neighborhood, the weather—all things that we were experiencing at the moment. It was a bond. Those days when the dew was particularly thick and the grass in the park was uncut, Joe picked Buddy up and held him on his shoulder.

Bob's dog was like a cousin to George, a rusty black mix of shepherd and collie. On election night in 2000, the four of us happened to meet at the far corner of the park. The news had just come in from Florida where, earlier in the evening, Al Gore had been projected to win that benighted state. Now the networks were saying there was a reversal. Florida was being taken out of Gore's column and it looked like it was going to Bush. Bob and his dog left his house at practically the same moment George and I left ours. We tramped around the edges of the park from opposite directions. When we finally met, we stood there together beneath the night sky in a shared state of disbelief. As we talked things through, the dogs lay down and waited.

In the weeks right after George died, I found myself getting up and going for walks around the park at night. It was like muscle memory. The trouble was I walked too fast by myself. The quality of my attention was different. What used to take twenty minutes now took five. I was also afraid I'd run into Barb or Bob or Joe. I wasn't ready for that yet. I quit going for walks and stayed indoors.

I'm glad to say that time passed long ago. Life, as they say, goes on. In many ways it's better. But I think Barb was right: I need to get a dog.

The New Public Library: The Beginning Is in Sight
May 9, 2007

There's been finger-pointing, red faces, and lawsuits, probably some ulcers, too. I'll bet there are people who probably wondered if the finish line for the massive Central Library expansion project would ever be in sight. The road taken to get here has been a well-documented mess; the legal and financial accounting, not to mention hard feelings, could take years to straighten out. But my guess is that when it opens this November, one thing will be clear: the new Central Library is the most impressive architectural statement made in this city in a generation.

One damned thing after another pretty much sums up the Central Library expansion story. From the discovery that the old Ambassador apartment building, sitting cheek-by-jowl with the library on the corner of Ninth and Pennsylvania, wouldn't be torn down, through cracked concrete in the underground garage, accusations about conflicts of interest in the awarding of contracts, and a tragic falling out with the expansion's architect, Evans Woollen, this has been a cautionary tale. A project that was originally budgeted at just over $100 million will probably cost close to $60 million more than that.

But now that the building is close to achieving its final form, a number of things are coming clear. For one thing, the presence of the old Ambassador turns out to be a kind of backhanded compliment. Like a garrulous relative, it prevents the library from assuming an air of splendid isolation. As you approach the library on foot from the east, its wall of steel and glass emerges magically over older rooftops. This juxtaposition of old and new reinforces the urban context and offers a glimpse of something people in Indy have too often shied away from—density. In this case, density means texture and surprise. We could use more of it.

Some people will doubtless complain that the expansion is out of scale, not just in relation to buildings like the Ambassador but, more importantly, to Paul Cret's classically inspired, and rightly beloved, original edifice. Evans Woollen, I think, has done a visionary job of preserving Cret's building, turning it into a symbolic portal into what amounts to a metaphor for how we understand knowledge in a digital age. His expansion rises up behind and above the old limestone building like Hiroshige's great wave. The message is revolutionary and unequivocal. What's wonderful is that Woollen found a way to honor the past without burying it.

The expansion's exterior is an elegant curve of stainless steel and glass. It's a statement in itself that has the authority to proclaim that Indy's downtown now has a new northern margin. For too long, downtown's practical boundaries have been subliminally defined by the Circle and its immediate environs. The new Central Library building creates the architectural equivalent of a northern anchor and invites us to imagine a host of new and active possibilities in its vicinity.

But the expansion's real power is only discovered once you venture inside. A couple of weeks ago I had the opportunity to tour all six floors. While it was still in a state of undress, I was able to see enough of what will be the finished product to be blown away.

A massive atrium connects the old and new buildings. It's an engineering feat of graceful, stemmed arches that, in their organic geometry, are worthy of the great Spanish architect Antoni Gaudi. Deep wood paneling has been used to warm the transition between Cret's limestone building, which will now be entirely devoted to the library's fiction collection, and Woollen's addition, which will hold everything else, including a 355-seat auditorium and more than seventy lending laptops that can be used anywhere onsite.

The scale here is grand, as it should be. Better, it's a grandeur that lifts you. Too often large-scale buildings make the pedestrians that step inside feel like ants. Sheer size is nothing more than a power trip designed to remind you that someone else is boss. Here, the scale takes you higher.

On the other hand, the stacks, while enormous in scope, create a sense of human scale. In part this is accomplished by doing without oppressive overhead lighting in favor of table lamps and illuminated units built into the shelving.

But what may be the building's greatest glory is its monumental windows, affording views of the city that have never been available to most of us before. By day, by night, and in all seasons, this will be the place to come to reconnect with one's visual sense of downtown Indianapolis. To be reminded that this is our city, our place, and what, in spite of all our faults and flaws, we're capable of. Here's hoping that, in future, when we gaze out through these magnificent public lenses, there are more buildings like this one to look at.

David Hoppe

Peekaboo Public Transit:
Riding the Super Bowl Shuttle
February 15, 2012

I'll remember the Super Bowl in Indianapolis for many things… The sight of people being pulled through the air by men who appeared to be toiling like galley slaves. Feeling crushed like a sardine Friday night on Georgia Street. Mayor Ballard chest-bumping Jimmy Fallon.

Most of all, I'll remember the glimpse, the teaser, the little peek the Super Bowl provided of what Indianapolis could be like with a decent public transit system.

My wife and I decided to ride downtown on the free shuttle bus that was taking revelers from Broad Ripple to the outskirts of the Super Bowl Village the weekend of the Big Game. We joined a cheerful group of pedestrians in front of the Vogue at 3:30 in the afternoon. There was about a twenty-minute wait before a bright yellow vehicle with room for about fifty riders pulled up.

It was nice that the shuttle was free, though the general feeling among our fellow passengers seemed to be that most of us would have gladly paid a couple bucks to be relieved of the hassle of having to find a parking space in the Mile Square.

What was really great about the shuttle was that it was an express bus, with nary a stop between Broad Ripple and downtown. After cutting up a residential street, we found ourselves taking a relatively scenic route that included stretches along the Central Canal and Meridian Street.

Once we got downtown, of course, all bets were off. The crush of traffic was such that, rather than wait until we arrived at our appointed stop, we riders pulled rank on our driver and bailed out—it seemed a few passengers, having quaffed a beer or two before boarding, were in urgent need of a comfort station.

So there we were, ready for action. I won't bore you with the details of our adventures, except to say it was pretty amazing to see so many streets that, most evenings, are barely populated, teeming with the genus Homo NFLerectus. We completed our fieldwork in a few hours and were outta there.

Shuttle buses departed from the curb in front of the Government Center. There we found a sturdy, good-humored fellow with a two-way radio who could tell us the whereabouts of the various shuttles, to Greenwood, say, or Mass Ave and Fountain Square, and when the next one was expected. The Super Bowl Village seemed to have a similar effect on many of us—it felt a little like what happens when a headache medication wears off—because we found ourselves waiting with a number of the same folks with whom we'd originally ridden downtown. Before long, all of us were climbing aboard for the ride home.

It was uncanny how natural the shuttle experience felt. Using a bus to better enjoy our city simply made sense. In Broad Ripple, of course, we're blessed with at least a couple of bus routes that can take us downtown with a minimum of fuss. But, as many of us know too well, service in most parts of Indianapolis is an arduous experience that scarcely serves workers, let alone evening pleasure-seekers.

The fact that Super Bowl planners recognized the need to embellish our dysfunctional public transit system says a lot. For a week, residents and visitors alike could get around in new and efficient ways. Parts of Indianapolis began to work like the big city where many of us have always wanted to live.

So it was ironic, if not downright disgusting, that at the very moment many of us were enjoying enhanced access to our city, members of the state legislature were killing a proposal that would have given people in Marion and Hamilton Counties the chance to vote to raise local taxes to pay for an improved public transit system.

It's a funny thing about Indiana politicians. As soon as they get themselves elected to anything, they conclude that the people who voted for them are idiots. How else to explain the oft-repeated reasoning given for denying us the chance to vote on this referendum: that allowing it to go forward risked linking politicians who backed it with support for higher taxes?

Never mind that the outcome of such a referendum would hardly be a sure thing. This is a city that overthrew a two-term mayor because he wanted to raise taxes to beef up crime-fighting efforts. While many of us have advocated for better public transit for a long time, arguing for the ways it can improve the economy, energize struggling neighborhoods, and contribute to a larger sense of community identity, it remains to be seen whether or not voters are ready to take this step.

That's why the glimpse we got during Super Bowl week of what a better public transit system could feel like was so valuable. For a few days, a lot of people who probably never ride buses used them to enjoy Indianapolis. It was, well, super.

Safe for Development: Safe from Democracy
March 15, 2006

It used to be so easy. Indianapolis, as someone once said, was "a give-away town." It wasn't just that everything here was for sale— hell, that was true most places. It was that it was so cheap.

But as we saw at the City-County Council meeting last week, that's changing. That meeting, you will recall, pitted a cranky bunch of chronic complainers, otherwise known as the people of Broad Ripple, versus condominium developers Kosene and Kosene and, it turned out, the powers-that-be in the city of Indianapolis.

Somebody must be losing their grip. That things were ever allowed to get to this point—I mean that the will of the people around here almost prevailed—well, it goes to show you: a little learning can be a dangerous thing.

How else can you explain a business-as-usual deal like this running into so much difficulty? Here you had Kosene and Kosene, ready and willing to ride to Broad Ripple's rescue. Why, they were so intent on saving that neighborhood they were willing to ignore the planning document approved by the Metropolitan Development Commission in 1997 that recommended limiting building in Broad Ripple to five units per acre or less. No, as far as K and K were concerned, that would never do. Instead, these heroic risk-takers would put twenty-eight units on an acre and a half. Dream no small dreams!

And so Kosene and Kosene politely asked for a zoning variance so they could go ahead with their plan to save Broad Ripple from itself. Needless to say, they expected no problems. When developers ask for zoning variances in Indianapolis, guess what? They get them over 90 percent of the time.

So imagine their surprise when they found that, instead of gratitude, their plans were met with disapproval in the very place the Kosenes care so much about—Broad Ripple. The Broad Ripple Village Association, an organization of Broad Ripple merchants and residents, came out against the plan. Then the Greater Broad Ripple Community Coalition, a group that was formed by residents who thought the BRVA was too soft on developers, followed suit. Yard signs, the tragic indicator of a neighborhood in decline, started showing up throughout the village, protesting over-development.

Undeterred, the Kosenes took their proposal before a hearing examiner for the zoning board. Incredibly, this public servant had the temerity to pay attention to the 1997 planning document and denied their petition. The Kosenes were then forced to appeal to the full zoning board, where force of habit was able to reassert itself with a 4–3 vote in the Kosenes' favor.

Ordinarily, that would have been the end of it. The Kosenes knew they could count on Broad Ripple's City-County Councilman, Jim Bradford, for support. Bradford's favorite animal, it's been rumored, is the bulldozer. But Joanne Sanders, councilor-at-large, lives in Broad Ripple, and she used her seat to "call down" the petition for a variance, in effect forcing the case to go before the City-County Council, a step that is rarely taken.

On February 28 a town hall meeting was called to order in Broad Ripple. More than two hundred people showed up. Although the Kosenes were not there, nor was Councilman Bradford, there were representatives from the Department of Metropolitan Development and the mayor's office in attendance. This was the first town hall meeting held in Broad Ripple in recent memory. The people there turned out by way of expressing their opposition to the favor K and K were trying to do for their community. The meeting was orderly, and public comments, while often passionate, were expressed in tones suitable for a family gathering. This appeared to be democracy in action.

That spirit carried over to the City-County Council meeting the following week. The chamber was packed with Broad Ripple citizens, who apparently had nothing better to do than go downtown on a weeknight to show how much they cared about their neighborhood. Among the people who spoke were the neighborhood's Republican committeeman, who said his canvassing indicated a vast majority of people opposed the development, and the head of Greenways, who said the development would encroach on the Monon Trail.

Luckily, cooler heads prevailed. It would have taken eighteen votes to stop the Kosenes building their condos. That effort fell four votes short. Once again, Indianapolis was made safe from democracy.

But let this be a lesson to us all, particularly in an election year. It's one thing to talk about the importance of citizen participation, about getting people off their duffs and into the voting booth. And it's all well and good to say we need better education, so that people will take the time to learn about things affecting their communities. But heaven help us if they actually do these things. They could make it awfully difficult for those who know better to go about the city's business, which, after all, is none of their business. Or is it?

Our Streets Suck:
We Get What We Pay For
March 30, 2010

These days it seems the whole world's apoplectic. As if fighting wars on two fronts isn't enough, we've been lobbing missiles into Libya. People are getting blown up (again) in Israel. The milk in Japan is radioactive.

Closer to home, the rich are getting richer while the rest of us are bankrupting the country. Apparently that's because we've got too many rights. And did I mention that the glaciers are melting?

When we are being ravaged by so much significance, it may seem beneath us to be talking about something so commonplace as the state of Indianapolis' streets. But I was driving around downtown the other night. As usual, it was a teeth-rattling experience. So I'm going to say here what I've been muttering under my breath for years: our streets suck.

I'm not talking about the crews that have been out industriously patching potholes recently. They, and Mayor Ballard's administration, deserve credit for making the city navigable.

But let's face it: the streets in this town are a mess. They're a patchy, cracked, and coagulated mass of civic denial symbolizing Indianapolis' unwillingness to get the most basic things right.

It's ironic that a city known the world over for hosting "the greatest spectacle in racing" is so careless at maintaining its roadways. You'd think that a community that's as car crazy as ours would insist on state-of-the-art paving. Then again, maybe this is a kind of safety measure, a way of keeping everyone's inner Andretti at bay.

But keeping our streets up to par would cost money. A lot of money, given the incestuous relationship between the contractors who do the work and the politicians who arrange to pay for it. It seems resurfacing a city street is a little like trying to sign a free-agent football player. The amount you have to spend is bound to be more than it should be. That may be OK if it wins you a championship, but it offends the Hoosier DNA when it comes to making civic improvements. Under these circumstances, we revert to our default mode and… do nothing.

Indeed, the inability to get our roads right isn't limited to Indianapolis. For years I've had occasion to drive Highway 12, a four-lane road connecting Michigan City, Indiana, and New Buffalo, Michigan. It's uncanny: even though both towns share the same weather, the Indiana stretch is always pocked and pitted; as soon as you cross the Michigan border, hey presto! The road becomes smooth. Must be that pesky time change.

It's not as though our elected officials aren't aware of this problem. Governor Daniels leased the entire Northwest Indiana Tollway in order to raise funds for infrastructure improvements. But this was the same Daniels who told a group last year that they should consider using a thinner grade of asphalt to cut costs on the I-69 extension. If they do, you can expect that road to never be finished. There will be crews out there patching and repairing great hunks of it for generations to come. Contractors call that a gift that keeps on giving.

For his part, Mayor Ballard is trying to find money for better roads by selling the water company to Citizen's Gas. As with leasing the toll road, cashing out a formerly public asset turns out to be a handy way of raising money without having to ask the public for a tax increase. In both cases, the public (us, in other words) seems comfortable with this kind of deal.

That's the trouble. We're the ones who elect these folks, so the blame for the deplorable condition of our streets really belongs to us. Ask most local politicians what's with the roads—or the sewers, the bridges, or the sidewalks—and they'll tell you how the buck has been passed from one administration to the next, going back decades. Nothing more than the minimum in road repair is ever done because we the people will punish the politician who tells us what it costs.

This says something about how we think about our city. It suggests that many people in Indianapolis are still uneasy about urban living, still wary about investing themselves in a place where the quality of life is determined by their willingness to be connected with one another. The city likes to brag about its volunteerism, but volunteers don't fix streets.

Lucky for us, we have an election coming this fall. Elections are great for streets. They affect mayors the way spring affects hibernating bears, creating sudden flurries of visible activity. For example, in a few weeks, they're finally going to start resurfacing Meridian Street. It's about time. Some cities have alleys that are in better shape than the outer lanes of this once-proud boulevard.

In scheduling this job for the months leading up to his re-election bid, Mayor Ballard is exercising a prerogative of his office, just like every mayor has before him. And to be fair, Ballard has paid more attention to streets than most. That just shows you how far we've let things slide; our streets still suck.

Is Local Food Trumping Art? Come and Get It
January 2, 2013

An artist was overheard complaining not long ago about the local restaurant scene. It wasn't that he was unhappy with the quality of what some of our better eateries offer.

What stuck in this artist's craw was what he perceived as competition. He pointed out that many artists in Indianapolis have a difficult time selling their works. While more people than ever turn out for First Friday gallery hops, and the quality of work on offer gets more interesting all the time, this has not translated into actual sales, even though many works of art can be purchased for a few hundred dollars or less.

What was getting the artist was his suspicion that a lot of the people who have been telling him they can't afford to buy his art were going to our ever-growing number of independent restaurants and spending their money on top-shelf cocktails, grass-fed beef, and free-range pork.

Local food, in other words, is trumping local art.

Or, put another way, local food is becoming our newest art form—and it's taking the town by storm.

Questions about whether or not food qualifies as art and, if so, what kind of art it is (visual? performance? conceptual?) have become an entertaining diversion in cyberspace. Author William Deresiewicz got the ball rolling with an essay in *The American Scholar* where he argued that "food has replaced art as the object, among the educated class, of aspiration, competition, conversation, veneration." But food, asserted Deresiewicz, is not art. That's because it "is not narrative or representational, does not express ideas or organize emotions, cannot do what art does and must not be confused with it."

It wasn't long before another writer, Sara Davis, responded via Drexel University's Table Matters web site. She said that asking whether food was art was the wrong question. After launching into a mini humanities seminar about what art is and how we experience it, she concluded by asking some questions of her own, all of which she answered in the affirmative: Can food be crafted with artistry? Can it convey meaning? Can food be a vehicle for inspiration for some of humanity's better qualities? And should it be taken seriously as a subject of study, a medium of expression, or a form of cultural exchange?

I am inclined to think that a meal, in the right hands or the right circumstances, can certainly provide an experience akin to what we're used to calling art. This is partly due to what's been happening in the food scene of late and partly because of how we have come to think about art.

Over the course of the past year and a half, I worked on a book about Indiana food called *Food for Thought: An Indiana Harvest*. The project allowed me the opportunity to talk to farmers and food artisans, master chefs and grill cooks all over the state. I found that very few of these individuals would describe themselves as artists. But, as they told me their stories, I also found the temptation to draw comparisons between them and the artists I know irresistible.

Like artists, people in the food movement—and a movement is what the burgeoning demand for what's fresh, local, and creatively prepared amounts to—tend to be individualists who marry hard-earned skill with a genuine love for what they do. Most of them see themselves as being part of a long tradition going back generations. They routinely risk material comforts and security to do something they find personally compelling. And that compulsion often has its roots in a desire to connect with something, call it a spirit, bigger than they are.

At the same time more and more of us are becoming increasingly discerning about the food we eat and how it is presented, our relationship to what used to be called "the fine arts" seems increasingly tenuous. Art, in the early twenty-first century, seems to be whatever anyone says it is. The Museum of Modern Art in New York, for example, has dedicated a gallery to an installation by Martha Rosler called "The Meta-Monumental Garage Sale," which the museum describes as "a large-scale version of the classic American garage sale, in which Museum visitors can browse and buy second-hand goods organized, displayed, and sold by the artist." What makes it "meta" or "monumental" seems to be the work's existence in a renowned museum, as opposed to, well, an actual garage.

It seems we want our art to be less about aesthetic artifacts and more about experience itself, with an emphasis on the social. In this formulation, cities where art happens are coming to resemble nothing so much as oversized summer camps. The artists play camp counselors, coming up with lots of activities to help us pass the time.

If this is true, then surely our best local chefs are artists who bring us together and illuminate, among other things, our sense of place through their use of locally sourced goods. In their hands, a meal becomes a kind of performance. And the restaurant where it takes place is, at once, a gallery and a stage. A place where every work exists in three dimensions, plus one: you can actually taste it.

Careful What You Wish For: Wooing Generations X and Y
March 8, 2006

The Great Beast, as Alexander Hamilton called the American people, is probably the most polled, analyzed, and researched animal on the planet. Lately, those parts of the beast's anatomy commonly known as Generations X and Y have been receiving special scrutiny.

In Indianapolis, that scrutiny has taken the form of a large-scale survey called "Developing Next Generation Arts Audiences." This survey was commissioned by the Arts Council of Indianapolis with funding provided by the Lilly Endowment; it was produced by a firm out of Madison, Wisconsin, aptly named Next Generation Consulting (NGC).

The survey was born of a felt need on the part of many arts and cultural organizations here to better understand how to attract adults between the ages of twenty and forty. These folks constitute the next wave of audience development. The problem is, they're not showing up in large enough numbers. What should be a wave looks more like a ripple.

Compounding this problem is the fact that Indianapolis has been paying attention to the ideas of urban economists like Richard Florida, whose research suggests that talented young professionals, the so-called Creative Class, are drawn to communities, not jobs, and that they place a high value on a lively cultural scene. The local embrace of Florida's ideas has been a boon for many arts organizations, resulting in increased public funding and a building boom.

But in making the arts an integral part of public policy here, there is also a new kind of pressure to perform. Implicit in the increased support for the arts is the expectation that our cultural resources will help plug the brain drain and make Indianapolis a destination for a new generation of entrepreneurs.

So where are they?

NGC studied trends affecting audience development in Indianapolis and across the country. It conducted focus groups of under-forty "high impact users"—people who attend ten or more arts events a year. A team of twenty-four local arts professionals was trained to conduct in-depth interviews with eighty-five diverse under-forties representing a wide range of different tastes and behaviors, and, finally, recommendations were developed "for the programming, formatting, and marketing needed to successfully attract and retain younger audiences."

The survey was presented to a gathering of arts professionals and advocates at the Circle Theatre on February 24.

Let it suffice here to say that "Developing Next Generation Arts Audiences" consists of two broad sections. The first of these addresses what younger adults are looking for when it comes to arts experiences. This is followed by a fairly detailed section on how to market via email.

At the Circle Theatre gathering, most of the questions from the floor concerned marketing and email. I hope this was more reflex than genuine response because the heart of the survey cuts deeper than that. According to NGC's findings, "the next generation wants to be engaged at a level beyond the art itself. The next generation wants a creative experience that includes learning, connecting, and/or sensing."

The arts, says the survey, are part of the new "experience economy." This means that it's not enough to simply sell a younger customer a seat; you have to offer opportunities for that customer to directly engage with other audience members, the art being presented, and the people who are creating it.

This sounds intriguing, but the report is woefully short on examples. Apparently many people who had seen Cirque de Soliel performances used that experience as a kind of shorthand for what they were talking about. Others mentioned having been moved by their visits to ancient cathedrals. And the Children's Museum came up frequently, too.

Perhaps the most interesting observation turns up in a supplement to the survey called "A Comprehensive Literature Scan," where the authors note, "Especially for the next generation, there is little discernment between arts and entertainment. Walt Disney was the grandfather of the experience economy...the Disneyification of American life have [sic] left young consumers craving side orders of entertainment alongside experiences ranging from retail to dining... and yes, to the arts."

This can't be good news for arts organizations whose understanding of their mission includes the upholding of certain traditions, the most notable of which may be the idea that art is something that happens in a plush piece of downtown real estate. Won't it be ironic if the end of all our building projects will be to discover that the next generation prefers its art site specific? That is, more fully integrated into the web and woof of the city itself.

Rebecca Ryan, the head of NGC, seemed to recognize that what the survey suggests might represent a pretty big gulp for some organizations. That it might be too much for them to swallow. Ryan reminded everyone at the Circle Theatre that there was no law requiring them to go after Generations X and Y. She said this with a straight face. She said it more than once. But she didn't mention the law of the jungle—and that's what this survey is all about.

When It Is Better to Receive:
Paying Artists for Their Work
December 21, 2010

It's the holiday season, a time when people come together around a variety of traditions.

I can think of one local tradition, though, that we can do without.

That's the Indianapolis custom of expecting the city's artists to work for free.

When it comes to the arts, this is a city that, in recent years, has learned to talk a good game. Everybody from the mayor on down can tell you—without having their arms twisted—about how the arts are good for downtown, contribute to the local economy, and attract smart people to live and work here.

We've even had our first serious dust-up over a piece of public sculpture, Fred Wilson's *E Pluribus Unum*, a statue of a freed slave proposed for the plaza outside the City-County Building. People arguing about art is better than ignoring it, which is the way things tended to be here for a very long time.

This is progress.

But Indianapolis continues to be a precarious place for artists to make a living. The most recent case in point concerns a request for proposals seeking works of art for the Indiana University School of Medicine's new Eugene and Marilyn Glick Eye Institute.

Funded in part through a gift of $30 million by the Glicks, this building will be home for the IU medical school's Department of Ophthamology. It is being touted as "a world class facility for patient care and research" that will "feature three floors of dedicated research space, giving IU clinical and basic science researchers the space needed to make discoveries that will help save sight and prevent blindness." The ground floor will house a clinic, where faculty members will see patients needing treatment for eye disorders like glaucoma, cataracts, and macular degeneration.

This is going to be a fabulous addition to the city. Better still, Ratio Architects, the firm designing the facility, will seek to have the building LEED certified for its energy efficiency, water savings, and use of sustainable materials.

The building should be completed halfway through 2011.

The request for proposals says that public art is being sought for the institute because, "It's important to have visual stimulation in a building dedicated to preserving eyesight and reducing vision impairments."

There's only one problem: "a budget is not available for purchased art at this time."

Even though the RFP goes on to assert that, "Spaces in the Eugene and Marilyn Glick Eye Institute have been designed to showcase art," zero dollars have been allocated to actually purchase any of the stuff.

The writers of the RFP actually rub it in a little by stating that donated funds are being spent on, "design, construction, interior furnishings, and equipment for research labs, clinical spaces and office spaces."

Everything, in other words, except art.

This, however, has not kept institute planners from asking Indiana artists (or artists with verifiable Indiana ties) to send them works of art at their own expense for possible display at the Eye Institute for a minimum period of six months. Artists whose work is selected for display must pay for shipping and provide proof that they are self-insured.

Wait, there's more: some works may be considered for eventual purchase by the Institute's Selection Committee. But: "If purchased, the value will be the fair market value of the piece, with 40 percent of the purchase price to be donated to the Eugene and Marilyn Glick Eye Institute."

You have to wonder if the folks who dreamt up this program

limited it to Indiana artists because they knew artists from other places—places, that is, where artists actually try to make a living through their art—would consider such a proposal insulting.

This is the way artists are all too frequently treated here. They are expected to work for free, or for the so-called "exposure" that being associated with a larger project supposedly provides. What most artists eventually discover is that exposure only makes you cold. It doesn't pay for heat or light or food on the table.

More important, exposure does nothing to create what the local cultural scene needs most, a genuine arts economy. For artists to reach their potential, their work—and it *is* work—must be practiced as a profession. Acknowledging that the arts are important is not enough. Builders must budget for them. For better or for worse, we live in a society that measures what's important in dollars and cents. Art that's not paid for is trivialized.

This is why building a percent for art into construction budgets, as is done in an increasing number of big cities, is so important. It prevents art from being an afterthought, while creating an economic platform for a city's creative class.

Seeing *The Tree of Life*: Art Minus a Money-Back Guarantee
July 27, 2011

My wife and I saw Terrence Malick's film, *The Tree of Life*, not long ago. It was an interesting experience.

Although it's been reported that *The Tree of Life* drew hoots and catcalls from the audience at its premiere at the Cannes Film Festival—before, that is, walking off with the festival's grand prize—the almost full house that we were part of at the Landmark Keystone Art Cinema maintained an almost preternatural silence throughout the film's 138 minutes. Sure, a few people exited shortly before the end.

But, given the elevated age of most of the moviegoers around us, this was easily attributed to the importunings of tetchy bladders.

Neither my wife nor myself are terribly talkative after we've seen something. We tend more to be a little dazed by the waking dream that even mediocre films and performances are able to conjure. This makes us terrible participants in the talk-back sessions that are a regular part of shows these days. We're usually halfway home before either one of us is capable of so much as a grunt, indicating that re-entry into the world of judgment has finally been achieved.

So we were taken slightly aback when a member of the theater's staff nervously pulled us aside as we were heading out the door. She asked if we'd seen *The Tree of Life* and if we liked it.

This, for reasons I'll get to in a moment, was not an easy question to answer. We responded as best we could at the time, saying that yes, we found the movie very interesting, in a good way. That such a qualification was, and is, necessary is a shame. How a word my dictionary defines as "arousing or holding the attention; absorbing" has come to be a social euphemism for "sucky" diminishes our language, but there you have it.

The staff member showed visible relief when we told her we didn't think *The Tree of Life* sucked. Then she confided that unprecedented numbers of people were saying they hated the film and were demanding their money back.

As a lifelong fan of the Chicago Cubs baseball team, the very idea of wanting money back for a disappointing exhibition of what is presumed to be talent in the service of a larger goal struck me as downright weird. Just as I would never dream of demanding a refund because my favorite team lost for the umpteenth time, the idea that a work of art might be held to the same standard as, say, a plumber's attempt to fix a leaky pipe suggested a deep disconnect between art and members of its audience.

The dimensions of this disconnect grew larger in the next few days. National Public Radio reported that *The Tree of Life* was drawing similarly hostile reactions in other cities across the country, including, of all places, Brooklyn, a haven for the so-called Creative Class.

Now let me say that I think *The Tree of Life* is a splendid and truly haunting film. Malick's ambition, to give visible form to memories, emotions, and knowledge that are often unseen, or barely glimpsed, is epic. As contemporary films go, this almost makes *The Tree of Life* a genre unto itself; compared to most movies, it's like a rosebush growing in a mushroom patch.

That said, I also found the film to be structurally flawed, laden with mystical excess, and in serious need of a sense of humor. The rumor that Malick may be thinking about unleashing a six-hour version of *The Tree of Life* makes me wonder if the Emerald Ash Borer doesn't have a point of view worth considering after all.

But as I said, these are things that make *The Tree of Life* interesting. I still have images from the film in my head, and, so long as I can see it on a big screen, I look forward to experiencing it again someday.

And what of the people who demanded their money back? I'm afraid their response represents what could be called the devaluing of art. In a world where people download music for free and watch movies on their iPhones, art looks more and more like ambient wallpaper. The fact that it's everywhere doesn't mean that anybody's really paying attention.

Just how we pay attention may also be changing. As what used to be considered works of art become part of our collective furniture, we become conditioned to certain forms and structures. Linear storytelling, for example—narratives with clear beginnings, middles and ends that are propelled by characters with identifiable arcs—are embedded in our brains. We can tune in at any point and tell what's going on, and this, rather than being dull, actually seems reassuring.

The Tree of Life violated some people's storytelling expectations. For them this meant the movie was defective, like a chair with three legs. The trouble—and the glory—of *The Tree of Life* is that it remains, stubbornly, a work of art. There's no way to fix it without ruining what makes it great.

Comedy for a New Generation
September 6, 2006

Sometimes comedy is as serious as a heart attack.

I was reminded of this recently at IndyFringe, the festival of alternative performance art on Massachusetts Avenue. The Fringe provided a platform for a variety of artists; I found the performances that stuck with me were delivered by a couple of the comedy troupes doing their thing at the American Cabaret Theatre.

The Cool Table is a group from Chicago, and Fresh Meat is a trio that hails from New York City. By and large, the players in both these outfits appear to be in their twenties. The result is that both groups tend to blast away with highly caffeinated sketches trading on the quirks and oddnesses of a generation seemingly trapped in the throes of arrested adolescence. There's plenty of yelling, a middle-school delight in cursing, and an ongoing wonderment about homosexuality equaled only by a complete and stupefying incomprehension of women.

There's nothing particularly new about this kind of schtick; in one form or another it has served as comics' bread and butter for generations. The Cool Table and Fresh Meat use it as a way of getting in the door, establishing solidarity with their peers in the audience. The beauty of sketch comedy, though, is that it allows you to turn on a dime, to take the audience from here to someplace altogether different in the blink of an eye. In some ways, it's an art of juxtaposition that enables artists to ambush audiences with disturbing ideas and observations. The Cool Table and Fresh Meat proved themselves expert at this. That's why I'm still thinking about them now.

About midway through their set, The Cool Table did a bit that involved a Vietnam veteran. Naturally, he was portrayed as being an older guy; Vietnam vets are old enough to be parents to the members of this group. It was a savage caricature that seemed, in a few seconds, to wrap every fevered stereotype from that war into a depraved ball and fling it at us.

As a middle-aged member of the generation that fought and protested that war, I found myself feeling uncomfortable at first. This sketch seemed to cross a line, not just of good taste, but of a way we've come to regard our history. The Cool Table sketch used a brutal kind of shorthand to make serious fun of our predilection for turning the people who survive the history we create into heroes or victims. I doubt an older person would have struck this unforgiving tone; I'm sure many people would, to put it mildly, consider it insensitive. But I found it liberating. We've spent years talking about "the lessons" the Vietnam War supposedly taught us. As current events have demonstrated—from the bitter candidacy of John Kerry to our self-aggrandizing willingness to destroy Iraq in order to save it—we've flunked the class. Sometimes it takes distance to see things clearly.

And then sometimes it takes being so close it feels like your nose is pressed against the windshield. Fresh Meat presented a slapstick sketch about a young woman on a job interview. She wants to be a "wardrobeal," a high-falutin' term we'll soon learn is a euphemism for coat check girl. The sketch was loaded with over-the-top physical comedy: an actor literally leaping back and forth across the stage. But at root, this was a piece created by and for a generation that's grown up hearing, as a kind of article of faith, that a college education is the ticket to a middle-class life as good, if not better than, that lived by their parents.

The young woman is told that although she has a college degree, she is not yet qualified to care for people's coats. It seems a lot of people are competing for this kind of work: she may have to go to graduate school.

The Fresh Meat sketch felt like a dispatch sent directly from the ranks of the underemployed. It begged the question: Who benefits from the fact that a college education costs more now than ever before, yet wages and salaries have been losing ground against inflation?

According to Fresh Meat, rather than answer this question, we've tried to distract ourselves by childishly puffing up to "professional" status what used to be considered menial labor. This sketch could have been dedicated to every person who works for $10 an hour and carries $20,000 in student loans.

In its stark assessment of today's world of work, the Fresh Meat sketch was as brutal as The Cool Table's take on our uses of history. It was telling, I thought, that neither troupe appeared interested in explaining themselves to an older generation, let alone courting their approval. Time's up, these comics seemed say: people have been talking about things your way long enough—and things aren't getting better. In fact, they're not even funny anymore.

Expanding Rings:
Life after September 11
October 11, 2001

Last night I dreamt I was in Broad Ripple on a sunny afternoon. I was standing on the sidewalk in front of the Parthenon restaurant on Guilford Street. I was looking north, past the fire station, toward the canal. Sun reflected off the white wall of the upper story of the Carter Building across the way with a Mediterranean intensity.

And then, without warning, that building exploded. A wash of debris blew past my face.

I write this by way of saying that, like a lot of people, I've been haunted lately. I'm only now beginning to realize how much. As has been noted here and elsewhere, the world changed on September 11. What changed, exactly, is another question. In New York City, the answer is obvious. There's a gaping hole where the World Trade Center once stood; a series of ever expanding rings encompasses the family and friends of the thousands of people who died there—and now, untold numbers more in Afghanistan.

The rest of America—the world, for that matter—has never seen as much of Manhattan as it has during the past few weeks. The first few days turned that city into a kind of electronic wallpaper all of us lived with for a while. Day after day and night after night, we were immersed in the apocalyptic montage: blue sky, white towers, and convulsive clouds of smoke intercut with faces, voices, the hopelessly indecipherable photos of loved ones taped beneath a striped pizzeria canopy. People began saying that we were all New Yorkers now.

This, of course, is not really true. For all its virtues, empathy has its limits. Those of us who experienced the events vicariously via the media were shocked and moved and angered, to be sure. For about a day, we weren't all New Yorkers so much as we were all Americans, sharing a national trauma. All of us got the news at pretty much the same time and in the same sequence, shared the same rumors, and, finally, closed our bleary eyes on the same wrenching scene. But this is a big country, and the next morning geography began to reassert itself.

The wreckage in New York City and at the Pentagon was screaming proof that change was upon us. In Broad Ripple, though, and in Irvington and Fountain Square, in Lockefield Gardens and Lockerbie, things still seemed pretty familiar. People I knew did a lot of sitting, quiet talking, absorbing.

Rarely has the difference between being there—and here—been as stark. For example, friends in New York have spoken about the gray, electrical smell that, for days, permeated the air. This is the kind of everyday detail that we, who live hundreds of miles away, can only imagine. We are no more New Yorkers than we are Afghanis.

And so we give blood and money for relief; we sit and talk, our sentences drifting off without completion. We stare at the blue midwestern sky, not so much watching as simply taking in that vast, incomprehensible space.

I've lived in Indiana for more than twenty years; most of that time has been spent here, in Indianapolis. The events of September

11 have made me want to focus with greater clarity on this place. In the first days after the attacks, I heard people say, with reason and relief, they were glad they didn't live in New York. Others said they felt safer here, literally under the radar. I can understand these reactions and even share them to some extent. But Indianapolis doesn't have to be on a list of targets to be affected by the fallout from actions taken miles, or half a world, away.

So far the crisis here is quiet. That doesn't mean our Islamic neighbors aren't in need of our support. Or that the laid-off airline worker next door isn't stressed. Maybe you know someone that's been called to active duty.

I remember the impressions Indianapolis made on my family when we first arrived here. There were the many unexpected courtesies and simple graces, like the cheerful inclusion of small children in otherwise adult settings and, most important, the first stirrings of friendships. This was a town with early springs and lingering falls, of old trees and gardens, of neighbors stopping in the street for a little conversation.

Our son was barely more than a toddler. On Friday nights my wife and I would walk with him into Broad Ripple for a Greek meal at the Parthenon. When the weather was warm, we'd sit at a table on the sidewalk and, as my wife and I finished our wine, our son would go exploring down the block, looking in shop windows and meeting passersby. Not once did we fear for his safety. The kindness of people he encountered gladdened us about the life of our community in ways we could never have imagined.

It's probably no coincidence that this was the setting for my nightmare. The explosion I dreamed about took place across the street. Yes, things have changed. The wheel of violence and retaliation is spinning quickly; we live with a new set of anxieties. This darkness, I'm sure, will pass. The job before us is to determine what endures.

Droned in Garfield Park
May 13, 2013

On a Saturday night not long ago, my wife, some friends, and I were sitting in Garfield Park, enjoying NoExit Performance's production of my play, *Our Experiences During the First Days of Alligators*. The title of this play is also its premise: without warning, alligators start turning up all over a midwestern town. The story concerns how a small group of characters adapt to these new, rather menacing, arrivals.

The play was about halfway through when we became aware of a dull buzzing overhead. It sounded like a swarm of angry bees. Just about everyone in the audience looked up to see what it was: a flying object, above treetop height, with four distinct corners, each tipped with red or green lights. The thing flew by, then it came back. It seemed to hover briefly, and finally disappeared. A friend sitting behind us leaned forward and gave voice to what all of us were thinking. "It's a drone," he whispered.

To their credit, none of the actors acknowledged the thing. The play proceeded without interruption. But during a Q&A session afterward, it became clear almost everyone there had been aware of this new arrival in our midst. It seemed all of us were struck by having experienced something for the first time: a *drone*. Drones, of course, have been all over the news. Much has been made of President Barack Obama's reliance on the military variety; he favors them for killing terrorists. Unfortunately, a lot of innocent bystanders in Pakistan and Afghanistan have suffered the consequences of this form of robot warfare.

Senator Rand Paul, R-Kentucky, drew attention to drones with his *Mr. Smith Goes to Washington*-style thirteen-hour filibuster. Paul said he was concerned about the government using drones to kill people here at home: "That Americans could be killed in a cafe in San

Francisco or in a restaurant in Houston or at their home in Bowling Green, Kentucky, is an abomination... I object to people becoming so fearful they gradually give up their rights," he said.

My wife Googled drones on the Internet. Right away she found a web site called uavdronesforsale.com where there were several drones that looked a lot like the one that buzzed us in Garfield Park. One, called the Aquacopter, a waterproof "quadcopter," was on offer for $350. Several were equipped with cameras for still images or video.

The market for drones, also known as Unmanned Aerial Vehicles (UAVs), has heated up since the all-but-unnoticed passage of the FAA Modernization and Reform Act of 2012. This calls on the Federal Aviation Administration to integrate drones into the national airspace by September 2015. The FAA estimated there could be as many as 30,000 drones being operated by public and commercial owners in this country in less than twenty years.

The FAA has granted 1,428 drone licenses to police, universities, and transportation departments since 2007. The so-called drone industry figures to generate about $82 billion in economic activity between 2015 and 2025. "We're not darkening the sky yet, but we're poised," said Richard Christiansen, the vice president of aerospace engineering for a firm called Sierra Lobo, at a California conference covered by Torey Van Oot of the *Sacramento Bee*. One doesn't get the impression Mr. Christiansen thinks this is a bad thing.

Businesses see drones as an easy way to help them to do everything from assessing real estate to delivering packages. And as with all new forms of technology, drone boosters see nothing but blue skies for their inventions. "There are smart people out there who when we put the technology in their hands, they're going to be able to think of great ways to use it that will save lives and protect property," said an optimistic woman named Kristen Helsel, who works for a company called AeroVironment.

Jason Goldman, identified by Van Oot as a recent grad from Pepperdine University and a drone hobbyist, enthused, "We're here now and we're ready. I say let us fly." The problem with flying, though, is that it means flying over something—like your backyard—or someone like you. During Indiana's latest legislative session, Sen. Jim Tomes, R-Wadesville, introduced a bill aimed at banning drone activity in Indiana. Tomes said he was worried about people's privacy and safety being compromised; he was also concerned about potential costs to taxpayers. His bill died in committee, and the Senate approved a resolution for further study.

According to the American Civil Liberties Union, legislation dealing with drones has been proposed in forty-one states, and enacted in Florida, Montana, Idaho, and Virginia. The ACLU urges folks to call on their legislators to support privacy-protective drones legislation.

Drones are just the latest version of a very old human story having to do with our penchant for falling in love with new technologies and the unintended consequences that shape the ways we live forever afterward. Booth Tarkington wrote about this in his novel, *The Magnificent Ambersons*. He told the story of how an Indianapolis family's life was flipped when the automobile made the carriage trade obsolete. In fact, he was writing about us all.

That was a Tarkington moment we had in Garfield Park. We were there to see a play; that drone is what many of us may remember.

The Butler Way: Still Buzzed
April 14, 2010

It's been over a week since the Final Four weekend, but I'm still buzzed about Butler. The games were electrifying. The "storyline," as the media liked to call it, was inspiring. The sense of community that rallied around the team was buoyant.

All this was great fun, a marvelous kind of entertainment made even more exciting by the way it unfolded in real time. But the public response to the Bulldogs, not just here in Indianapolis, but around the country, suggests that the Butler story resonated with people in a way that was bigger than basketball. For once the clichés about how sports can sometimes show us more than what it takes to win or lose, but something like a way to live, came true.

In the newspapers and on TV, a lazy shorthand developed to try and describe this feeling.

At first, Butler was referred to as an "underdog." This is one of America's most popular designations. It means that someone who's not supposed to win—someone who's not big or rich or powerful, lacking the usual advantages—can still come out on top. The great jazz bassist and composer Charles Mingus called his autobiography *Beneath the Underdog* as a way of saying his journey began with even less than nothing.

We love underdog stories. They're democratic parables about how supposed experts can be wrong and odds don't have to matter. Underdogs remind us that wit and determination can be the bootstraps we use to pull ourselves up.

Butler's small student body, emphasis on academics, and comparatively low athletic budget made it an underdog. Occasionally one sports pundit or another would mildly dispute this label, pointing out that Butler entered the NCAA men's basketball tournament with a high ranking. But the ranking, it turned out, didn't mean much when it came to the experts' perceptions of Butler's chances. Always, from one game to the next, I never saw a sports pundit pick Butler to win. They were wrong until the very end, and then they were just barely right.

After its ecstatic Saturday night victory over Michigan State, Butler became David to Duke's Goliath. This brought the underdog theme into focus, giving it a biblical patina. David, of course, was the shepherd boy who downed the towering Goliath with a well-placed stone from his slingshot. Asked how he liked having his team compared to the diminutive David, Butler coach Brad Stevens smiled and said this was fine with him because, "David won."

As we know, David, er, Butler didn't win the national championship. They came within a second and a shot of making it happen. The remarkable thing is that when the game was over, Butler's fans weren't crestfallen or bereft the way fans usually are when their vicarious hopes are dashed. Never has defeat felt more like victory.

We often console ourselves with platitudes that emphasize process over product, the journey over the destination. We know there is wisdom in looking at things this way. That wisdom, however, is a lot more satisfying when those processes and journeys have a payoff. Had Butler lost, say, in the Sweet Sixteen or the Elite Eight, the impact of what they accomplished would have been a satisfying vindication of their process—it would also have been down to size. But this time the story—a run that literally lasted until the last second of the last game—really did matter more than the outcome.

As the tournament built to its climax, more and more was made of "The Butler Way," a set of five principles the basketball team uses for self-governance. Those principles are humility, passion, unity, servanthood, and thankfulness. Together, they amount to a recipe emphasizing the team over the individual player, a determination to face reality and make the most of it using the tools at hand.

As the tournament unfolded, it became clear that the Bulldogs were putting the principles of The Butler Way into practice. And so, yes, they were underdogs, yes, they seemed a lot like David, but they also stood for something that rang true to a growing number of people.

It wasn't just that Butler's basketball budget is small—$1.7 million compared with Duke's $13.9 million. In a world where we've been conditioned to believe that you grow or die and that progress equals always getting bigger, Butler showed limitations needn't preempt excellence.

It's nice to think that Butler's achievement owes something to midwestern character, a modesty that is no less rigorous for its preference for a well-rounded life defined more by what it includes than by the single-minded devotion to someone else's definition of success. We see this in Coach Stevens' insistence that scholarship and team-work necessarily reinforce each other.

But Butler's story is relevant wherever people see the virtues of the local, the handmade, and human scale. It's about how what you get your arms around can actually contain a world of meaning.

Colts, Bears and My Friend George: Football Rules This Weekend
January 31, 2007

My buddy George called from Chicago to tell me all the ways the Bears would beat the Colts to win the Super Bowl. He said he liked the fact the oddsmakers were picking the Colts to win by a touchdown. This, said George, will give the Bears an edge.

George is my oldest friend in the world. We've known each other since before our kindergarten days. Now George lives in a con-do on Lake Michigan; if he feels like it, he can go down to the street and walk along a boulevard that's named for his great-uncle, the late, great George S. Halas, Papa Bear himself.

But we grew up on the same block in a northwest suburb called Mt. Prospect. We played a lot of sandlot football together when we were kids. For us, football season started with the high hay fever of late August and lasted until there was snow on the ground in De-cember. George was the quarterback and I was the wide receiver: the split end we called it in those days. I remember one New Year's we celebrated with me going out for a pass at midnight and George hitting me with a perfect spiral atop a snowbank.

George's dad scouted the Green Bay Packers for the Bears, which was a big deal since the Packers and the Bears had such an in-tense rivalry. Every couple of years he'd supply George with a genuine

NFL football, the kind the pros used. It was real leather and smooth, not pebbled like the ones you got at the sporting goods store.

It was fun being just a degree of separation away from the Bears. I have to admit, though, that it made me a little jealous. It was also frustrating because the Bears were known for their running game; they didn't have a standout pass receiver I could look up to. That's how I came to be a Baltimore Colts fan.

The Colts had the legendary Johnny Unitas at quarterback; Raymond Berry was his favorite receiver. They were the Manning and Harrison of their day. People talked about how Unitas threw to Berry along the sidelines when the Colts beat the Giants in the 1958 title game, a game some said was the greatest ever played. I had a picture that I cut out of *Sports Illustrated* with Berry sailing flat-out through space, catching a pass on his fingertips.

Before the start of every football season I would write to the Colts in Baltimore and request their latest yearbook. They would send me a copy for free, and I would pore over the contents, reading about Berry and Johnny U., Gino Marchetti and Billy Ray Smith, John Mackey and Bobby Boyd. One year I wrote to Raymond Berry. A couple of weeks later I got a postcard from him that I still have today.

Time passed, of course. George's family moved out of the neighborhood, and George and I went to different high schools. We lost touch with one another—and, for awhile, I lost interest in football. Not long after that, the Johnny Unitas era ended for the Baltimore Colts. The team was sold to Bob Irsay, the man who would bring the Colts to Indianapolis.

The fact the Colts were in Indy meant nothing to me when I moved here in 1988. Like a lot of people, I thought the Indianapolis Colts were pretenders, a team without a real tradition. Unlike the Bears, their games were rarely sold out. And they played in a dome, an unnatural act, as my friend George, who has braved the elements to watch not just the likes of the sublime Walter Payton, but the ridiculous Cade McNown, can tell you.

Needless to say, my attitude about the Colts began to change when Peyton Manning came to town. Like the great Johnny U., Manning calls his own plays. He turned the Colts into a kind of jazz band: a well-rehearsed unit able to improvise at the drop of a hat. The Colts are happening again, and if their midwestern edition is still a little wet behind the ears tradition-wise, that's ok. A win this weekend will do wonders.

Speaking of which: after adventures too numerous to mention, George and I picked up the thread of our boyhood friendship a few years back. Hence that phone call I mentioned. George, I have to admit, has always known more about football than I do. But when it comes to the Bears, he's also a cock-eyed optimist, the kind of guy who sees a tidal wave coming his way and thinks it's time to open a surf shop. He thinks the Bears have the Colts' number.

We'll see, George, we'll see.

Indy Wears It Well:
Bringing Home a Championship
February 14, 2007

It's been more than a week since the Colts' victory over Chicago in the Super Bowl. We've had our first real snowfall since then, state legislators are still scratching their heads over what to do about property taxes, and a few of the Pacers again tried their best to give our city a reputation for after-hours fun rivaling, say, East St. Louis.

Life, in other words, has gradually gotten back to normal around here.

The Colts, though, have proven themselves to be the best football team in the land, and this gives our local version of normal a gloss it never had before. After Bob Sanders intercepted the Bears' hapless quarterback for the last time on Super Bowl night, you could practically feel our frozen city melt with relief. And the next day, when the team was welcomed by tens of thousands at the Dome, the frigid air was suffused with gratitude.

Other teams, the Colts included, had made it to a national stage in the past. None, though, had managed to bring home the prize. The Colts made football history in Miami, but they added an exclamation point to the continuing saga of this city. It was a kind of gift.

Under these circumstances, it's tempting to be smitten by the Colts. Last week, after returning from Miami, the mayor felt it necessary to issue a proclamation calling on everyone to keep wearing blue and showing their Colts colors as a way of demonstrating their continuing support for the team. As if the Colts' self-esteem needed a boost. The mayor came off sounding like a homely guy who can't believe he's just gotten lucky with the hottest girl in school.

It's true: Indianapolis is lucky to have a professional sports franchise as classy as the Colts have turned out to be. Jim Irsay and Bill Polian have done a remarkable job of building an organization based on loyalty, dedication, and honest effort. In Tony Dungy, they've found a coach who exemplifies these qualities and in Peyton Manning, a prodigious talent to lead the way on the field.

But you can't help but think that the Colts have also been lucky to find themselves in Indianapolis. Sure, this is a small market; players may not benefit from some of the perks associated with bigger cities, but they're not under an in-your-face microscope, either.

In the two weeks leading up to the big game, the Chicago press went out of its way to make fun of Indianapolis. We had pie, they said—and the Colts—but what else? When Chicago's Mayor Daley deigned to make his bet of city goods like deep-dish pizza with our Mayor Peterson, Chicago pundits wondered what Indianapolis could possibly offer.

There was no real way to answer those slights. Indianapolis, with apologies to the hardworking folks at the Convention and Visitors Association, is a great place to live, but I understand why many people wouldn't think of visiting. Pinning down what this means, exactly, is tricky. The shorthand way of talking about it is to refer to our "quality of life." But that's not to say there still aren't plenty of neighborhoods in this town that need a lot of work, or that too many people here are in distress with no clear way out.

In a way, it was perfect that the game wound up being against Chicago, our big, bruising cousin on Lake Michigan. For years Chicago has been tagged "the second city." The chip on its shoulder over this has been as big as its ambition to prove that it's a world capital.

Indianapolis is more modest. For whatever reason, we're not comfortable with the kind of ambition that pushes its way into rooms and demands attention. In Chicago good manners are a sign of weakness; here, they're part of how we create space for one another. Many observers have noted the humility that seems to be at the core of Tony Dungy's way of dealing with the world. That's a characteristic that fits Indianapolis, where Dungy has become a quiet hero.

On the night of the Colts' victory celebration, we left the Dome a little after eight o'clock. From the top of the stadium steps we could see snow covering the roof of St. John's church, where the carillon played "The Battle Hymn of the Republic." We followed the crowd downtown—kids whooping and hollering for joy, their breath making clouds above the sidewalks. Then we got in our car and drove north on Delaware Street. In minutes we were on the Old Northside, passing venerable trees and glowing porch lights. We'd found the heart of another winter night in Indianapolis. It felt familiar. It felt grand.

Swinging Away at Sandlot Indy:
Rediscovering a Pastime
July 16, 2008

Marty Sterrett has the look of a kid in a candy store. Sterrett is an active-duty firefighter in Lawrence, but he's also a lifelong baseball fanatic, a guy who has not only loved but played the game for as long as he can remember. That look on Sterrett's face is thanks to the new business he's gotten himself into, something called Sandlot Indy.

The Sandlot Academies are a national franchise offering state-of-the-art facilities for people who want to improve their baseball and softball skills. At Sandlot Indy you can pay $35 and for a half hour find yourself facing the equivalent of a Big League pitcher who, in addition to throwing a lot of nasty breaking stuff, can freeze you with a 100 mph fastball.

You want to know what it's like to face Kerry Wood—without, that is, the possibility of getting plunked in the ribs? The closest most of us are likely to come to this boyish fantasy is the batting cage at Sandlot Indy.

Like Marty Sterrett, I got hooked on baseball just after I learned to walk. Most games were played in the daytime then, so the background sound of the daily radio play-by-play was as common a part of the summer soundtrack as someone cutting grass or the spit-spit-spit of a lawn sprinkler.

I spent hours bouncing a tennis ball off the steps in front of my house to practice my fielding. And most days there was an informal game going in a field down the street that began in the morning, broke for lunch, and resumed in the afternoon. When my Dad got home from work, we'd play catch.

If, in those days, baseball seemed like a bigger deal, maybe that's because the sports business was smaller. Sports, and baseball in particular, were beloved pastimes, but the games were never considered to be more than games. A great thing about going to a Big League ballpark was that you saw everyone there—from hustlers and touts to bank presidents. The cost of a ticket was easily affordable, good seats were usually available, and the players themselves were accessible, willing to sign autographs and even answer fan mail.

On any given day, somebody won, somebody else lost, and life went on.

All that's changed. We've turned our games into mythic, larger-than-life symbols that supposedly impart messages to us about who we are, where we live, and what's worthwhile. In the process we've turned athletes into millionaire celebrities and sports franchises into publicly funded utilities that, ironically, are too costly for most members of the public to actually attend. Living off this spectacle is the media, who often seem to devote more time to the analysis of off-field dealings than to the games themselves.

How out of balance has our sports mania become? Newspapers across the country are cutting space they used to allocate to arts coverage and laying off writers who wrote about everything from classical music to theater to movies. Sports sections, meanwhile, are all but untouchable, and sometimes, as in the case of a steroids scandal, an institutional implosion ala Indiana University, or a star-struck tryst between the likes of the Yankees' A-Rod and Madonna, reach as far as the front page.

Now sports, like any form of popular mythology must, has a dark side.

This is too bad because I don't think sports were ever meant to carry this load. Yes, certain matches and games can and do reach a level of high drama. And yes, there are individual athletes who, on occasion, actually affect the outcome of events through a force of will. Memories are made of this.

But, for the most part, sports are about making things simple. They reduce the otherwise dismaying complexities of life to basic terms: throwing a ball, catching a ball, hitting a ball.

So it did my heart good when Marty Sterrett handed over a bat and invited me to make a fool of myself at Sandlot Indy. Suddenly the daily grind was a long way off. "You'll want to see the 100 mph fastball," he said with genuine enthusiasm. "Everyone does." It's been a long time since I've tried to hit a baseball. Based on my attempts at Sandlot Indy, it'll be a while yet. But the kid in me was glad to swing away.

The Livability Challenge: A Game Changer for Indianapolis
October 20, 2010

In sports, that's what they call a play that tips the contest's momentum. With a single stroke, the underdog takes the lead.

Indianapolis may have had a game changer of its own last week. The city was site and subject for a three-day workshop called The Livability Challenge, a national project sponsored by an organization called CEOs for Cities, an alliance of urban leaders from across the country supported by the Rockefeller Foundation, working in collaboration with Brian Payne of the Central Indiana Community Foundation and Tamara Zahn of Indianapolis Downtown, Inc.

The workshop brought a team of nationally recognized city planning and design gurus together with local business and civic leaders for a sequence of intensive sessions aimed at coming up with principles and projects to enhance Indianapolis' quality of life.

The working premise behind the CEOs for Cities initiative is that the twenty-first century is the urban century.

A large and ever-growing majority of Americans live in cities. This means that the country's identity is undergoing a transformation from a land of wide open spaces and cowboy individualism to a model that's more like a mosaic: interconnected, blended, and dependent on an array of moving parts. According to CEOs for Cities, the

American Dream is becoming an urban dream.

An idea like this one packs an extra wallop in Indianapolis. This is a city with a love-hate relationship with urbanity. You see this in our lack of public transit, miles of low-slung sprawl, and our penchant for allowing suburban-inspired architecture and windy surface parking lots downtown.

At the same time, though, Indianapolis is poised to become a model for what it means to be a mid-size city in a post-industrial age. As one of the visiting gurus noted last week, this city "has good bones." Our problems with air and water quality and infrastructure, while significant, are not intractable. Our scale is still human-size.

The Livability Challenge sessions revolved around this statement: "Our ambition is to make beauty, in the form of art, good design and nature, always present."

For those of us who live in Indianapolis, this statement contains several game changing elements worth unpacking.

In combining "art, good design and nature," this statement emphasizes the extent to which city life is something we humans create and need to manage. In a city, even nature is managed—or it had better be. Left untended, it becomes toxic and disruptive, a force that can shatter the web of connections that make city life sustainable.

But we're after more than sustainability. By creating systems enabling nature to thrive and bloom, we also make a place that informs, inspires, and can even heal us. Combining art, good design, and nature is also important for Indianapolis because it finally acknowledges the importance, the necessity, really, of including artists, designers, and green advocates in the discussion about city planning. This has nothing to do with being artsy-fartsy. It's about finally bringing the kinds of expertise to the table that, throughout history, have moved cities forward, adding value that transforms the lives of individuals, families, and communities.

But the biggest game changer of all is this statement's use of the word "beauty." Beauty, believe it or not, has been a real bugaboo in the art and design world for over a generation. Somewhere along the line, the culture vultures who determine what's hot and what's not, got it in their scavenging skulls that beauty was too easy, too accessible, or somehow unjust. To say that something was beautiful was obvious. And if it was obvious, it couldn't be important.

For all this highfalutin' theorizing, beauty still gets the last word. Beauty moves us. Unless the game is rigged, beauty wins.

Making beauty the governing principle in how we think about city livability is a bold move. Its practicality is breathtakingly sensible. It begs the question: Where would you rather live, in a beautiful place or an ugly one?

Think about how our city, your neighborhood, might feel if that question were asked every time a decision was being made to build something new or tear something down, widen a street or make way for power lines.

Words matter. The language we use to talk about things makes a difference. Putting a word like beauty at the heart of how we talk about livability creates a space where everyone can feel free to participate.

Of course, there's a great distance between the intentions expressed at the Livability Challenge and what might actually occur. Money, as always, is an issue: conferees recommended the city use $400 million from its sale of the waterworks to leverage public-private partnerships and fund projects. Mayor Ballard was in the room when this came up. Whatever he was thinking, he kept it to himself.

But as participants talked about what they had experienced and wanted to do, it was hard not to think something different was afoot. It was like watching a pass interception in the fourth quarter, a fresh team taking the field. Could be a game changer.

Getting Married: Here's to the Future
March 20, 2013

Our son is engaged.

To be married, that is. He called us a few nights ago. Before telling his mother and me the news, he made sure we were both on the line; his mother held her breath in the kitchen (she had a feeling this was coming), while I (clueless) hustled upstairs to pick up the extension.

Something like pandemonium erupted.

By our reckoning, Graham and Amy have been together for about five years. They met in college, where they traveled in the same circles; then they were friends, who managed to navigate the various iterations of today's courtship rituals, including moving in together and moving to another state.

Now this.

All of us know how fraught marriage has become. It's almost as risky a proposition as opening a restaurant. Something like half the couples who agree to marry wind up getting divorced. That's what happened to me the first time I tried it. I can still remember sitting alone with the judge in his office in the county courthouse as he signed the no-fault papers. It was late in the afternoon on a bone-chilling day in early spring. When he was finished, the judge looked at me in a way I would like to think of as kind. In that moment we were like two characters in an Edward Hopper painting; there was nothing left to say.

Graham's mother and I will celebrate our thirtieth anniversary this June. I am at a loss to account for our good fortune. All I can say is that hardly a day goes by I don't thank my lucky stars I had the presence of mind to ask her to marry me. And that she said yes.

Like Graham's mother and I, Amy's parents are long married. I am told that when Amy offered them the news over the phone, Graham could hear the whoop of joy from across the room. I can't help but think this makes some kind of a difference, that if the mothers and fathers in this story were living apart in different towns, different states—geographic and otherwise—their feelings, while no less loving, would surely be tempered somehow by bittersweet experience.

As it is, the prospect of this impending marriage feels tidal, like the natural movement between and across generations. Our family histories make it possible for us to celebrate it as both a distinct moment in time, one to be gathered round and savored for itself, and a continuity, another turning of our mutually familial wheel.

A dear friend of ours, twice divorced himself, asked why anyone today would feel a need to marry. I doubt there is a need, as such. We've known couples that have made long and rich lives together and never needed vows. Perhaps it's the word "need" itself that's a culprit here. You shouldn't get married out of need, and need is certainly not enough to hold a marriage together in any true or nourishing way.

The wanting to be married must run deeper than the imperative to scratch a certain itch. For some of us, it's a family thing, but it's a community thing, too. Marriage is an opportunity to stand before whomever it is we consider our tribe in order to acknowledge that two of us are crossing a threshold. It doesn't matter how old we are, where we've been, or what we've done, getting married is a way of finally declaring ourselves adults.

No wonder then so many same-sex couples want to participate in this. Laws supposedly intended to "defend" marriage by forbidding some of us from tying the knot actually do little more than consign an entire class to a state of perpetual relationship adolescence. As countless Internet dating sites attest, it's hard enough for two people to find each other in a way that matters in this world. What's crazy is that, so long as we have this thing called marriage, we try to prevent some of us from being part of it.

Marriage, of course, is also a way of believing in the future. But even that has become a loaded proposition these days. There was a time, not that long ago, when the idea of progress was a palpable thing. Standards of living improved from one generation to the next, as surely as day follows night.

Well, we're not so sure about that now. It seems we work more and earn less. Even a college degree isn't what it's cracked up to be. As for the planet, we keep pushing it harder, making more demands. We know we're doing damage, finding it in the air we breathe, the water we drink, hiding deep inside us.

As Rick tells his lover Ilsa in the movie *Casablanca*, the problems of little people like us don't amount to a hill of beans in this world. Under the circumstances, it can be easy for marriage to seem like just another pale gesture.

Or its defiant opposite. Because when two people get married, they show us a way forward. In this, Graham and Amy, bless them, are leading with what is best about us all, their hearts.

Leaving the Old Neighborhood: Broad Ripple Farewell
June 13, 2013

We sold our house yesterday.

Houses are sold every day. Some folks do it as a kind of pastime. They buy a place, get bored or restless, and sell. Before the housing bubble burst, this was a great way to make money. Maybe it still is.

But that's not our story. This was the first house we owned, and we lived there for twenty-three years. For my wife and son and I, it feels now as if those years flew by. Talking to people, though, I get the impression this is a pretty long time to stay put.

We had our reasons. Chief among them was the neighborhood.

We lived in a part of Broad Ripple called Broadway Terrace. It's on the west side of College, in what amounts to a kind of enclave bordered by the canal towpath, Central Avenue, and Kessler. This is the "other" side of College, the side away from the Village nightlife, and although we were not immune to the occasional bit of drunken misadventure, usually just after closing time, my guess is that being on the far side of that thoroughfare made for a better night's sleep.

Broadway Park is the heart of this neighborhood. It's what might be called a pocket park—less than three acres. But it has tennis courts, a sandy lot for volleyball, a picnic shelter, and what's called a spray pool—a constellation of jets, some mounted overhead, that shower kids (and the occasional overheated adult) with cascades of water.

I thought of Broadway Park the other day when the Trust For Public Land's report on urban park systems came out, ranking Indianapolis forty-seventh among fifty cities. Only about a third of us live within a ten-minute walk of some kind of green space. Being able to have a park that close to home may seem like a lot to ask in a city the size of Indy. But I can speak from experience: it makes a difference.

The park was like our backyard. It wasn't just green space; it was breathing space. Kids laughing in the spray pool provided our ambient sound on summer afternoons.

It was also a social space, especially for dog walkers. Neighbors might see one another two or three times a day. These encounters often led to conversations. I remember running into my neighbor, Bob Timm, on election night 2000. Both of us were accompanied by our pooches, Cumo and George. We met twice that night. The first time, early in the evening, it seemed Al Gore had things well in hand. Then, later, it seemed the vote in Florida was going the other way. George W. Bush was on top. Bob and I muttered in the dark by the edge of the tennis court; it felt as if the country had just fallen overboard. Our dogs settled patiently in the damp grass and waited for Bob and I to vent.

The park, of course, attracted its share of miscreants. If you live in a place long enough, you see cycles come and go, including the occasional spasms of illegal activity. My wife and I were awakened one winter night by the colorful whirl of mars lights on our bedroom ceiling. We opened the curtains to see a pair of police cars blocking the intersection in front of our house—and another neighbor, radio personality Big John Gillis, looking for all the world like legendary wrestler the Great Zbyszko, stripped to the waist, wearing only his pajama bottoms, frog-marching a hapless burglar down the middle of the street. I don't know who was more nonplussed by this spectacle, the burglar or the cops.

Time passing also means losses. Last year we walked home from our favorite Broad Ripple restaurant, Ambrosia, to find an ambulance parked in front of Big John's house. Neighbors Tom and Alissa Prather stood by Sherry, John's wife, while paramedics tried unsuccessfully to save him. John had lent me his copy of Kurt Vonnegut's last novel, *Timequake*; just days before he'd knocked on our door to share a bit of local knowledge and told my wife, "Gosh, I'm glad we're neighbors."

I could go on. There was that time when my dad died; we had to leave town for a week, and Craig and Denise Bush, the couple across the street, volunteered to look after our dog. When we finally returned, there was Craig, mowing our front yard, our dog watching him as if this was all in a day's work. Craig shrugged off my thanks, telling me he figured yard work was the last thing I needed to be doing just then.

Or how about the mural Alissa and Rebecca Hens painted on that carport along the alley by the park? They and their husbands, Tom and Rick, got tired of looking at something ugly and made it beautiful, in one afternoon.

You take away a lot when you live in one place for twenty-three years. And though the time has come for us to move on, I'll be forever grateful for this neighborhood. It's amazing: the place is in the middle of a great city, there are lights everywhere, and yet, on a clear night, if you look up, the sky is full of stars.   Finis

About the author . . .

David Hoppe has been a writer, editor and columnist for NUVO, Indianapolis' alternative newsweekly, since 1998. He has received nine awards from the Indiana Society of Professional Journalists in a variety of categories, as well as a Creative Renewal Fellowship from the Arts Council of Indianapolis and a Time-Life Creative Writing Fellowship. Hoppe is also author of the book, *Food For Thought: An Indiana Harvest* (Indiana Humanities) on that state's burgeoning food scene. He has edited two collections of essays, *Where We Live: Essays About Indiana* (Indiana University Press) and *Hard Pieces: Dan Carpenter's Indiana* (Indiana University Press). His professionally produced plays include, *After Paul McCartney* and *Our Experiences During the First Days of Alligators*. A selection of his writing can be found at www.davidhoppewriter.com.